Songbird
A Nightingale Story

A.S.Chambers

To Sue
All the best :

DEDICATION

For all those out there who are thrown into situations that at first seem unsurmountable, yet they find the courage deep down to not only survive but thrive.

ALSO BY A.S.CHAMBERS:

Sam Spallucci Series.
The Casebook of Sam Spallucci - 2012
Sam Spallucci: Ghosts From The Past - 2014
Sam Spallucci: Shadows of Lancaster – 2016
Sam Spallucci: The Case of The Belligerent Bard – 2016
Sam Spallucci: Dark Justice - 2018
Sam Spallucci: Troubled Souls – Due 2019
Sam Spallucci: Bloodline – Due 2020

Short Story Anthologies.
Oh Taste And See – 2014
All Things Dark And Dangerous – 2015
Let All Mortal Flesh – 2016
Mourning Has Broken – 2018
Hide Not Thou Thy Face – Due 2019

Ebook short stories.
High Moon - 2013
Girls Just Wanna Have Fun - 2013

Omnibuses.
Children of Cain - 2019

Contents

Orphan   1

Servant   13

Daughter   39

Sister   55

Regent   85

Author's Notes   95

ACKNOWLEDGEMENTS

Many thanks to the fabulous Liam Shaw for bringing Nightingale to life in his amazing cover art as well as giving more than just a hint of construct.

Also, as usual, big thanks to Theresa Main for being my second pair of eyes in typo spotting.

Plus a big shout out to all those who backed this book through Kickstarter. You guys are amazing. Thank you very much.

"There will come a day when they will be ready…
When that day comes, I shall return."
Justice - *Family*

"The life of a Child of Cain is more likely doomed to be
one of misery, sorrow and death."
Marcus - *Sam Spallucci: Dark Justice*

Orphan

Okay, so let's set certain things straight from the word go. This is a vampire story. Of course it is: I am a Child of Cain. As such, I was created to perform three tasks.

Find the Eternals.

Protect the Twins.

Await the Divergence.

Three little tasks. You'd think it would be simple, wouldn't you?

Quite.

Anyway, those are my purposes in life. (Is it life? I guess I'm technically dead, but you know what I mean – I'm still living, from a certain perspective).

So, like I was saying before my little existential diversion, this is a vampire story, teeth and all. However, please don't expect the following:

Steamy sex scenes.

Incest.

Necrophilia.

More steamy sex scenes.

Lots of hovering around in shadows, stalking my ex.

Scantily clad female vamps with cleavages so vast you could sail ships on them.

Steamy sex scenes with the aforementioned above.

I'm just not that kind of girl...

The first time I was born would have been about a hundred and sixty years ago, give or take. I can't say that I remember the event, being just a few seconds old.

Unlike the second time I was born.

Remembering the day that you came wailing and bleating into the cruel world of Victorian England wasn't something that really mattered in my family. What did matter was staying alive, especially after my father died. I was old enough to remember his passing, but not really of an age to fully comprehend it. One day he took to his bed, then, after what seemed to be a very long time in a small child's eyes, he went a funny colour and just stopped. The look on his face after he dies is one of my earliest memories. He was lying there, the plain white sheets pulled up close around him in his pale fingers, a look of pure bewilderment on his face. It was as if he had reached the end of a mystery novel and the murderer had proven to be someone who had been hardly mentioned, or had walked in right at the last minute.

It was the look of a man cheated.

Needless to say, my mother took it very hard. She had always been a quiet woman, industrious in her housework, but after my father's bemused slipping away, she hardly ever said another word to my brother and me. We just knew that we were expected to perform our chores whilst she struggled to make ends meet. I'm guessing that she must have held down numerous jobs in order to feed us and it was probably the constant work, work, work in those appalling Victorian conditions that finally did for her. After about ten years or so of drudgery and silence, it was just me and my brother, Jacob.

He was a bit older than me but not once did he use this as means of belittling his sibling. "Esther," he said, the day after our mother was buried on top of god knew how many others who had also perished in poverty, "it's just you and me now, isn't it?"

"That it is."

"We must do what we must to keep each other safe, 'cos we're family."

That was what he was doing when he ran out in front of a cab. A shop keeper had been chasing him for thieving some beef and he hadn't been looking where he was going. The horse ran right over him, apparently. The wheels too. The impact broke his neck and he died instantly.

I was left on my own, my family gone.

So, at some year which was apparently in the 1800s, the century when the country in which I lived felt that it ruled the world, I was of an unknown age with a disturbingly fragile future. I decided that I was certainly not going to sit around and wait for one of two inevitable fates: prostitution or death. I realised that the village where I had lived all my days, Irlingbury, was probably not the best place to earn a living, so I turned my sights up to the bright lights of the largest town that my young self knew.

Wellington.

It took me a day or so to walk there, seeing that I had no money and could not afford a more luxurious form of travel, so when I reached my land of milk and honey (or least an honest day's work) I was so tired out that I was only vaguely aware of my increasingly urban surroundings. All there was that stood out above the hurly burly, the clattering of hooves and the shouts of market stall holders was a gothic spire that strained up from the middle of the town, attempting to pierce the grey, soot-saturated sky above.

So it was that I decided I might as well start there in my quest for employment.

"Are you a Jew?"

The man sat at the rather fine desk (looking back, it was probably mahogany — all I knew back them was that it was wood) was probably the most

5

severe looking person I had ever come across in my short life. He was dressed in a long black vestment (I later discovered that this was a cassock). At his neck was fastened a white collar that came down a short way in two strips of cloth. He was almost completely bald; just a vague fringe of white hair ran from one ear to the other, circling the back of his otherwise bare head. A pair of small, wire-rimmed spectacles sat atop his hawk-like nose. From behind these lenses, a pair of grey eyes lanced me to the spot where I stood in front of his desk.

"Well, are you?"

"I… I don't know what one of those is, sir. Is it some sort of a servant girl?"

The clergyman leaned forwards, steepling his pale fingers. "First," he instructed me, "you will not call me sir. You will call me Vicar. Second, Jews are possibly the furthest things removed from servants. They are lazy, slovenly heathens who claim to be the true children of our God above, yet had the barbaric audacity to crucify His son."

"Very good, Vicar."

He nodded, then leant back in his chair which creaked against his weight. "Tell me, why are you looking for work here? I have not advertised for a servant girl."

"I need an income, Vicar, and the church was the first place that I really saw. I said to myself that a building that size must always be in need of an extra pair of hands, so I thought it a good place to start looking for work."

His eyes narrowed. "You say that you require an income. You must be no more than eighteen. Have you no husband to support you? Have you no father?"

"I have neither, Vicar. I am an orphan."

"A waif and stray. Tell me, how should I be assured that you will not steal my silver? How can you be trusted? I cannot imagine that you have in your possession any letters of recommendation."

"No, Vicar, I have none. But I am an honest girl."

He snorted and threw a copy of the newspaper that he had been reading across his desk at me. I caught a glimpse of an extremely graphic printed sketch on the cover and averted my eyes from the gruesome details that it illustrated.

"I'm sure that young woman felt that she was an honest girl." It was impossible to miss the scorn in the cleric's voice. "Honest to her clients and those whom she serviced, until some deranged lunatic slit her open in a back alley."

I kept my eyes averted as he mercifully stowed the paper away. "Was... was that round here?" I stammered, my legs shaking beneath me. I began to dread that I had brought myself to a monstrously dangerous place.

"No, thank the Lord," he said. "Some hellhole holiday town up in the far north. Nothing like that ever happens here."

I forced my legs to quit their trembling and I

regained my composure. "I assure you vicar that I am truly honest. And I am a hard worker."

He stood from his chair and moved around the desk before circling me. I stood still, facing forwards, afraid to let my eyes follow him.

"So you say. Yet the Devil often speaks what the sinner wishes to hear. These could just as well be lies and deceit." He paused behind me. I imagined those grey eyes studying me, trying to peer into the depths of my heart. "How can I be sure to trust you?"

I took a deep breath and summoned all the courage that I could muster. "Why not set me a challenge: something which would prove my worth. Make it an arduous task to prove my strength and ability, yet make it something which will also prove my trust."

There was silence for a while as he pondered this, then he said, "Very well. Follow me."

I think my jaw must have dropped when I entered All Saints for the first time as my potential employer snapped, "Don't gawp, girl. It does not become you."

"Sorry, Vicar. It's just that… well, it's the most beautiful place I've ever seen."

And it truly was. You have to remember that I had come from abject poverty. Jacob and I had owned just the clothes that we had worn. We had possessed no house to call our own, sleeping in alleys and doorways once mother had passed away to be with our father once more. My life had been one of mud, filth and scraps. All Saints sang of something completely otherworldly. The wooden pews faced in regimented order towards the front of the nave where an ornately carved wooden screen traversed the width of the building. Atop this was the most lifelike carving of a man that I had ever seen. Sadness filled his silent, bearded face, his eyelids closed in calm serenity as his arms stretched wide on a wooden cross.

"Is that Jesus?" I asked, my eyes not leaving the carved simulacrum atop the rood screen.

"That," snapped the cleric, "is a thing of idolatry and, if I had my way, I would have it stripped from this place of worship and burnt to ash. Our Lord is with his father in Heaven and does not need things that spurn His righteous commandments in order to worship Him. However, it was donated by a family that have certain weight hereabouts and their regular donations would soon dry up should I offend them."

My eyes travelled to the opposite end of the nave and I frowned as I walked over to a plain metal bowl that sat on a simple table. "Do folk have to wash themselves before they're allowed in here?"

"Are you sure you're not a Hebrew?"

I glanced back at the vicar and he sighed in acknowledgement of my genuine ignorance.

"That, dear girl, is a font. It is a bowl we use to cleanse the sins from those who come to seek

9

forgiveness of their Lord. Once they have been washed clean, they are fit to serve Him."

I stood before the basin and reached out to it in fascination. There was something that drew me to it, something that I couldn't fully comprehend.

The priest must have noticed my curiosity. "You will hear all manner of nonsense regarding the history of this church," the cleric continued. "Some will prattle on that it was once a heathen place of worship where people came to be healed by a magic spring. You are to disregard all such superstitious stories. It is a house of God: no more, no less."

My eyes remained fixed on the plain bowl. It was so small, so unassuming yet... Was that the sound of rushing water that I could hear in the distance?

"So, what is the task that you wish me to perform?"

It took me over five hours. I knew this because there was a huge clock outside, under the spire of All Saints, which was accompanied by a carillon of bells to chime off every quarter hour of my Herculean task. Just as six in the evening called out to the citizens of Wellington, I climbed up off my knees and surveyed the fruits of my labour. Every single pew shone in the fading light of the day that weaved its way through the stained glass up above. My cloth was near worn out and my tub of beeswax nigh on empty.

What was more, seated on a stone step at the foot of the rood screen was a small figurine; a delicately carved representation of a woman holding a young infant in her arms. I placed my hands in the small of my back, stretched, then bent down and picked up the statuette. It was the most delicate object that I had ever lain eyes upon. The features of the pair were exquisite — the mother looking down adoringly at her smiling babe. Truly this place was a treasure house of wonders!

Right on cue, as if he had been watching secretly from some unknown vantage point, the vicar entered the church and walked up behind me. "It seems that you are hardworking and trustworthy after all. The pews gleam and that little treasure remains. You could have easily walked out of here and sold it for a reasonable sum that would have fed you for months, you know. It is extremely old."

I looked down at the figurine then up at the rood screen before back to the clergyman. "I think that perhaps either eventuality would have been welcomed by you."

"How might that be?" He relieved my hands of the statuette as he raised an eyebrow.

"On one hand, you gain a trustworthy servant. On the other, you would have been rid of an embarrassing piece of idolatry that you could not otherwise have disposed of."

A small smile touched his lips. "Why don't I show you to your quarters?"

A.S.Chambers

Servant

I never realised that the way the vicar treated me was unacceptable.

Why should I have done? I had known nothing else. Life had taken away my father, my mother, my brother and, in doing so, had driven me into the destructive orbit of a total sadist.

It wasn't like he ever laid a finger on me.

He was far too clever for that.

I had seen my fair share of abuse in my short life as a human girl: men drunk on cheap ale beating seven bells out of their spouses for daring to answer them back; starving teenagers being dragged along shit-ridden streets by the scruff of their filthy jackets to the local well-fed magistrate; a small dog kicked to death by its owner for refusing to eat the noxious scraps that had been thrown to it.

I was never on the receiving end of anything so immediately violent from the vicar of All Saints, but I was abused over and over again, nonetheless.

I guess I was just too glad to have a place to sleep and to not be out on the street, whoring myself to the nearest man who looked like he had a few coins to spare for an hour of meaningless fornication. In my innocence, I probably thought that the verbal repudiation and physical punishments which I received were duly meted out and that I needed to learn from my mistakes.

Not once did I realise that he was a fervent believer that every being had their place and that his and his wife's stood firmly above mine.

The best way to describe his spouse was as a viper presenting itself as a Siamese cat. She appeared as a reserved and dignified mistress of the house. She dressed simply, but her clothes were undoubtedly of good quality. They lacked the usual frills and frivolities associated with the Victorian social climbers that one saw around town, yet they were smart and hung well upon her. There was neither lavish lace nor sumptuous silk. Her clothes were made from more practical and hard-wearing materials, befitting her and her husband's religious beliefs. When her husband entertained members of the diocese or the county, she played the perfect hostess, flattering them and preening their egos. However, when she was out of their line of sight, it was clear from her eyes that she found them totally contemptible.

I, on the other hand, received more than just withering looks.

As the only member of staff in the house, I was the sole recipient of her constant demands and whims: floors to scrub, wood to polish, tea to be served. And not once was it ever remotely satisfactory. There was always a spot of dust that I had missed, or a teaspoon incorrectly placed. Her favourite phrase was, "Well, I suppose a blind man would like to see it," and there were many more similar comments besides. Due to the lack of frills and bustles on her clothes, my mistress made very little sound as she prowled around the vicarage, seeking signs of some misdemeanour committed by my obviously sinful hands. I was constantly on tenterhooks, aware that she could appear over my shoulder at any moment, either in the house or the church. I had to be constantly on my guard as I was never fully sure whether she was around or not. She apparently went out socialising a fair amount. I had no idea where she went when she left the vicarage and I wasn't really bothered about finding out - I just enjoyed getting on with my chores in a relative peace and quiet.

And what a litany of chores that I had to perform!

In the morning, I was to rise promptly at five and ensure that the vicarage was spotless. I was to do so in such a manner that did not cause my master and mistress to wake from their slumber. I was to polish the furniture, sweep the floors, light the fire. Once that first round of tasks was complete, I was to prepare breakfast for the vicar and his wife, which they would receive in the dining room at seven forty sharp. There would be eggs, some toast and marmalade, tea. My employer was a firm believer that meals should be frugal and efficient. Once one erred to the side of sweet pastries and the like, then one became slovenly, fat and incapable of performing a decent day's work.

His decent day's work involved morning prayer in the church, followed by all manner of parochial business to which I was not privy. Should I enquire, I would be met with a firm wall of silence.

Once he had departed on his duties, I was then allowed to have the first of my two meals for the day. Bread.

And I was to be grateful.

Songbird

After the Word of God, bread was our prime sustenance. Bread was sacred due to our Lord consecrating it at the Last Supper. Bread fed those who worked hard and deserved their place in Heaven.

I reminded myself of this as I ate my solitary slice at ten every weekday morning.

Once my repast was consumed, I was to turn my attention to the church itself. Again, floors were to be swept, woodwork was to be polished and glass had to be washed. The building remained open from morning prayer until said evensong every day. So it was that people often drifted in and out of its cool, meditative surroundings, be it to wonder at the beautiful architecture, grab a moment of silent prayer or just shelter from the wind or rain. On no account was I to talk to any of these visitors. I was to remain silent, fastidious in my duties and just politely nod if they ever spoke to me. Gossip was the tongue of the Devil; I was under strict instruction to never allow it a voice.

Said evensong was at six in the evening, after which I was to serve the vicar and his wife their evening meal. Once a week I went to the surrounding market to buy in provisions which were charged to his various accounts. He never trusted me with money, even though I had previously shown that I was not a common thief. On these days, I had to work twice as hard in my cleaning duties to make up for my time away from my chores. When he returned home from evensong, I was to see to it that his evening meal was ready and waiting for him. It was to be a meal not repeated within seven days. This was because each day was a gift from our Lord as he laboured on every single one except for the Sabbath. Each day saw Him undertake a different task of creation, so each day I should serve a different meal to celebrate this.

They would finish dining around half past seven of an evening, after which I cleaned and washed up, finally free of my duties by around eight. At this time, I was allowed to fill my plate with the remnants of the food from their dinner and feed myself. I was to have no more than that which filled the plate, as this was to remind me of my position and I was not to succumb to gluttony like so many young women did these days.

I was to be abed for nine and asleep within half an hour, ready to resume my duties at five the next day.

It was a busy life. I was overworked, underfed, but I had a place to sleep and a roof over my head. Who was I to complain?

From what I recall, it was when the hacking, painful cough would not go away that I realised things were bad. Very bad. However, looking back on it, there had been numerous other warning signs: instances that had screamed, "Run away, now!"

The first was down to something as simple as a conversation.

"Did you clean all this on your own?"

The voice made me jump. I had not heard anyone enter when I had been at the far end of the nave putting the finishing touches to the polishing of the pews. In my head, a beautiful tune was ebbing and flowing across my brain, drawing me into its embrace. I'd had no idea what the melody was or from where it had originated, but it was wonderfully relaxing, serene. It felt like the first light rain on a warm spring day and it helped to keep me fresh as I toiled, sweat rolling down my back.

Not that I was permitted to sing along to it.

I almost banged my head on the back of the pew as I knelt up with a start. A dark-haired, neatly dressed woman was stood at the end of the row, near the small, plain font. She was looking straight at me.

I frantically cast my head from side to side, looking to see if my employer was in the vicinity. I dared not break one of his rules. Only that morning, he had decided that his breakfast had been lacking and had burst into a rant about how the lack of effort in one's work was one of the sins of Ninevah, leading to a proclivity towards sloth and gluttony.

The woman leant her head to one side and granted me a curious look through her dark-rimmed spectacles. "Ah, you are not allowed to talk to strangers." She sat down at the end of the pew, her finely tailored clothes not demonstrating so much as a crease. Her eyes faced forwards, towards the rood screen and, more specifically, the cruciform figure that hung upon it. "So, I shall sit here and perhaps I shall talk and you will just listen? Agreed?"

I was still nervous, but it seemed acceptable. I was not technically breaking a rule. I could carry on with my chores whilst the woman talked. I nodded as I resumed my polishing of the woodwork, albeit with somewhat less attention than before. There was an entrancing nature about the woman that made me want to listen to every word she said.

"It's funny how places change yet intrinsically remain the same," she mused, her eyes not once leaving the crucifix. "I used to come here regularly as a young girl. The lad I was courting was in the choir; I guess I just drifted into the community alongside him. I was never really a churchgoer, but this place drew me in. Like it does so many others."

She rose noiselessly from her seat and I watched her walk towards the centre of the nave, where north, west, south and east meet. She bent down, removed a fine leather glove and let the tips of her delicate fingers touch the cold, stone floor. "I miss that young man so much. He gave everything."

I couldn't help myself: "Was he killed?"

Her reply was no more than a whisper. "Worse."

Then, for an instant, I was aware of something most strange. My senses seemed to deceive me as I heard muffled shouting. I spun my head around, thinking it was the vicar, but we were still quite alone, even though I could distinctly hear the tones of a male voice shouting in the church. The words were obscured, unintelligible, but they carried anger amongst them. Then there was the sound of metal on metal, a clashing sound of... swords?

But this was nothing compared to what followed.

The noise that seemed to fill the church was something that I could not comprehend. It was a roar, a shriek so primal, that my guts turned to jelly. It sounded like a number of beasts of hell screaming out as one, before launching a deadly assault.

Then there was peace.

Then there was sorrow.

I looked at the dark-haired woman and saw that she was crying — a solitary tear caressing her pale cheek. As she wept, I was aware of two things.

First, was the tune in my head from before — crescendoing, wrapping itself around me, encompassing me and lifting me high from this place, through the stars, across countless galaxies.

Yet all the while I was still stood here, watching this curious woman demonstrate her reserved grief.

The second was an accusatory shout. "Girl!"

The music fled, back to whatever shadow it hid within and the lonely tear miraculously evaporated from the woman's cheek as the vicar stormed out of the organ chapel and into the nave.

"You are supposed to be working," he scolded me, "not bothering those who come seeking solitude."

"Sorry Vicar," I whispered, snatching up my cloth and returning to my duties.

"I am so sorry, my dear," he fawned upon the visitor. "My maid is ignorant and does not appreciate that the faithful require space for their prayer and contemplation."

The woman eyed him up and down before throwing me a quick glance. "Sir, I believe that your young girl appreciates far more about this place than you ever could." With that, she turned her back on the cleric and walked out of the church, leaving me alone with my employer.

That was the first of many nights that I was made to sleep outside.

It rained and I was soaked through by morning, but this did not concern me that much for, with every drop of blessed water that struck my chilled skin, I heard note after note of the tune that had reached out to me that afternoon. I let it lift me from that dreadful place and transport my soul across the skies and stars.

It soothed me that night and many more to follow.

The Vicar was what these days is referred to as "low church". He had no use for, and indeed abhorred, all those things that he referred to as "papist trappings": incense, vestments, Latin. He also disapproved of singing. "When the sinner sings," he said sipping his tea one day, "he provides a portal into which the Devil may enter."

"What about the hymns we sing in church?" I asked.

"They are different," he explained. "Those are spiritual words that are full of good intent. When we praise our Lord, He smiles down upon us and blesses us."

I tidied up his tea things and just nodded, pretending that I understood the difference.

Personally, I thought it was poppycock. Especially when the church was full of such a beautiful song, even when there was no one there to sing it.

I didn't hear the wondrous music all the time, or perhaps I did and I was just not fully aware of it, but it was always present when I stopped to take a breather from my chores. The song was lilting, flowing beguilingly through the pews, along the nave, around the church, hovering over the font. It was enticing, infectious, summoning. Once its notes had danced into your ears, it was impossible to ignore. It would begin as a simple three note, repetitive melody that whistled for you to come, remove your burden and join the dance. Then, once it had your attention, the harmonies would begin to weave around each other. From the highest soprano to the lowest bass, the tune wrapped you in its arms and rocked you, soothed you.

It remained with you when you left the building. Once you walked across the threshold, you were aware of an emptiness within your body as you stepped back out into the mundane world of street vendors, hucksters and cabs, but there, in the recesses of your head, deep down inside your ears, those three simple notes still resonated.

It was those three notes that I was humming when the vicar heard me.

I was preparing his evening meal. It was a broth of beef, mutton and carrots. "Simple food for a simple man," he would have said. As I chopped the vegetables and prepared the meat, there they were, the trio of notes dancing around in my head; their arms out, calling me, beckoning me to join the dance. I resisted, because I knew that, should my employer catch me, I would be in severe trouble.

But they were so insistent.

Over and over they called to me, motioned to me with outstretched hands: "Come join us. Dance with us. We are alone. We are everywhere. We have no one."

How could I resist?

I was hardly aware that they had left my lips, lips which smiled with glee at the feel of the beautiful little tune that was being hummed over and over. As I chopped the carrot, I felt the notes lifting me off the ground once more, carrying me across a great river that encircled my world. I became aware of other voices joining in with the words — throngs of voices.

Not human voices.

The beings that my mind saw joining in with my chorus wore robes of white and bore feathery wings on their shoulders. Angels.

They sang louder and louder, higher and higher.

And above all the voices, one was more strident, more beautiful than the rest. There, in the midst of the angelic host, stood one being far more magnificent than the others. He was adorned with not two but six resplendent feathered wings, outstretched to their greatest extent. He radiated the most intense light, brighter than a million suns and in his fiery hands he held a chalice and a sword.

And, as he sang, the three notes formed into intelligible words…

"We are one!

"We are one!

"We are one!"

"What in God's name are you doing girl?"

I was dragged out of the highest heaven, down through the spinning galaxies, across the river that snaked its way around creation, back into the small kitchen where meat and vegetables bubbled and boiled.

Down into a heap of trouble.

"Vicar," I blurted out, "I'm so sorry! I did not realise!"

"Heathen child!" He stormed, his face reddened, his eyes on fire. "How dare you disobey me? How dare you commit such a sinful act?"

"I'm sorry! I'm sorry!" I continued to apologise. "It was just a little tune."

"A little tune? You stood there swaying as if you were a harlot on a street corner seeking to seduce some innocent young man with more money than sense! Come with me. Now!"

He stormed out of the kitchen. I removed the vegetables from the heat and followed him, terrified to not obey. He marched out of the house and into the garden; I scurried along behind him, my stomach lurching with fear. Was I to be shut out again? Was I to be treated no better than a dog?

We processed over to the church. He unlocked the door to the vestry and ushered me inside. Once inside the cool building, he marched me down to the back of the nave, to the font. "You need to be cleansed," he growled, "washed of your infernal sins. Stand here." He pointed to a spot next to the small basin. "Bow your head."

I did as I was commanded and awaited my punishment.

It came in the form of words and water. The vicar launched into an ad hoc service of baptism. He rambled on about sinners needing to be bathed in the River of Jordan just as our Lord had been many years ago. He barked questions at me to which I nodded a terrified response and he poured water over my brow from the small font. It could not have lasted more than fifteen minutes, but I was so scared, my stomach undulating madly, that it seemed an eternity.

"And now," he whispered, his voice low, threatening, "you will stay here the night and you will pray upon what you have done. You will accept that you have been cleansed of your sins and you will ask our Lord to guide you and prevent you from following the Devil any more. Do I make myself clear?"

I nodded, my movement no more than a hesitant judder, and he stormed out of the building, leaving me alone, wet and shivering, in the dark.

But I wasn't alone. Not really.

At first I knew not what to do. I stood shaking in the cold darkness by the small font, baptismal water trickling down my face and my neck. I didn't think I had ever been so scared. I thought that I must have been terribly, terribly wicked to make the vicar so irate.

I shuddered as I felt a chill skitter down my spine and I coughed harshly into my trembling fist.

Then I heard the music once more.

"Go away," I whispered miserably. "Please.

Leave me alone."

But the notes grew in volume, and with them, the sound of water, rushing like a sea inside a shell.

I walked away from the font, to the centre of the nave, the spot where the woman had knelt, and I curled up on the floor like a small babe, unsure as to what I should do. As I did, I heard the music increase in volume once more and the voice of the six-winged being crying out above all others, calling to me. I shut my eyes tight, wanting to be far away from this place, but the song crept inside of me, warming me from the cold night air. It stroked my heart, filled my belly and pumped my lungs so that I had to open my mouth and the notes came, once more, from my voice.

All the time, I lay there on the floor, my eyes closed, curled up in a ball. There was just me and the song, nothing else.

We were all that was. I was the tune and the tune was me. It wrapped its arms around me, encircling me, embracing me like the truest of lovers. I felt its hands caress me and its breath upon my skin.

My brain frantically tried to rationalise this insane situation.

How could a song be alive?

How could a mere tune be tangible, be in possession of a physical form?

The questions were truly valid, but ultimately unanswerable. Instead, I remained entranced, my eyes shut and my senses exhilarated at the miraculous thing that could not possibly be.

And I opened my mouth.

Such sounds that came from within me, I had never notioned to be possible. It was my voice, my breath, of that I was sure, but the actual noise, the melody that flowed across my tongue was the words of a being that I did not know. A being far, far older than I. A being that was lonely and in need of comfort.

We are one!

We are one!

We are one!

And we were. I was truly one with this entity, drawn into its sublime nature, all physicality disposed of and disregarded.

That was, until I felt the water lapping at my face.

My eyes snapped open and the sight I saw made me sit bolt upright.

There was a lake of water around the nave of the church. It was washing up the side of the pews and swirling towards the rood screen. My head snapped from side to side to locate the source, which it did. There, under the font, clear water was surging up from beneath the floor. At first it was a casual flow, but then, as I stared in stupefaction, the water performed the impossible. It rose from the floor, swirling around the small bowl in a spiralling column, rising up into the air, gaining in momentum.

And, as I watched the sea rise from the earth below, I could swear that within its watery midst there was fire; small balls of energy flashing and zig-zagging in amongst the rising waves, which grew faster and faster in whirling velocity.

And, all the time, the three notes rang over and over in my head, filling my soul, escaping up through my vocal cords and out through my mouth. My head was jubilant and my heart ached for more.

And more there came.

The water pulsed and shot upwards towards the roof of the church. Grasping the font in its aqueous grip, it punched through the woodwork and out into the night sky as the song reached its climax and stars exploded within me.

Then, as if someone had placed a snuffer over a flaming candle, the anthem was gone and the water fell, cascading down into the nave and smashing the pews aside, ripping them from the stone floor.

I should have been fearful, terrified at such destructive power, yet I just stood still, unaffected, as the nave was ripped apart around me. I remained calm in the eye of the violent storm, as water parted round me and not a single thing struck my body nor did me harm.

Then, it was over and I was stood alone in the carnage.

That night in the church earned me a week of sleeping outside.

I have to admit that I was amazed that he did not just dismiss me; it would certainly have been easier. I guess that I just did not realise that the vicar was the sort of man who craved power over others. He was actually enjoying watching me suffer.

His wife, for once, made no comment, no barbed remark, but there was no mistaking the fact that she took great delight in me sleeping outside in the cold and the rain.

Not that I was able to sleep.

Every time I closed my eyes, the otherworldly symphony would resume. The three notes rising and falling in a breathless susurration, a rhythmic accompaniment to the rattle that was slowly increasing in my aching lungs. Then, as the moon rose and the stars above twinkled, the words would come once more and I would see the six-winged, fiery figure standing above me still clasping his sword and chalice, his arms outstretched like Jesus on the cross. But there was no sorrow in this creature's face.

There was joy.

There was satisfaction.

This was someone, something, who did not know suffering or, if they did, it had been so long ago that the torment had been purged from its memory. This was a being who was at one with itself, true to its purpose. In my increasingly fevered dreams, it looked as if his sword was piercing the sky and matter from beyond the stars was flowing through the wound, pooling into his chalice.

"We are one."

Those words haunted me, comforted me, taunted me, guided me through the long, long nights. Silently, for fear of being heard, I mouthed them over and over, a mantra, a prayer, to calm me through my exile from my bed.

An exile that lasted seven days.

There was no explanation, no apology (not that I ever expected one), not even any further punishment. Just three different words. These ones were far more mundane: less oblique.

"We have guests."

And with that, I was ushered inside to the bathroom where I was left alone to make myself presentable, a maid fitting to respectable members of parochial society.

My legs ached and my fingertips were chilled as I brought tea through to the study, yet I knew better than to reveal my discomfort. Instead, I concentrated on the task at hand, kept my head down and provided refreshment for my employer and his two guests. One was another cleric (his cassock and dog collar instantly gave that fact away), the other was immaculately presented in a finely tailored grey suit, sporting a pair of pince-nez and a well-groomed head of hair.

"The fact of the matter," Mister Pince-nez was saying, his hands held out in a placatory manner, "is that there just aren't the funds available."

Vicar was sat behind his desk, his grey eyes lancing the suited man to his own chair. Not a word escaped my tormentor's mouth. His anger was palpable.

As he did not bid me to go, I decided that perhaps I should stay awhile and catch up on matters.

Pince-nez squirmed under the pressure from the ocular lance. "It has been a very harsh year. The diocese has spent much money on good deeds to the poor. It simply does not have the funds nor the resources for a building undertaking such as this. The financing will have to come from the parish."

No wonder my employer was cross. In my mind's eye, I saw the cataclysm that had befallen the church and I shuddered at the cost.

There was an exceptionally awkward silence in the room.

Pince-nez continued to squirm.

The other cleric sat quiet, reposed. Just another day; another trivial matter.

"Tell me," Vicar finally said, his words barely controlled, "why has my Lord Bishop not seen fit to come and tell me this himself? I invited him here to witness the destruction of the building, to show him just how we cannot possibly afford to rebuild it."

Pince-nez swallowed and opened his mouth to speak, but the other priest lay a hand on his colleague's shoulder before standing and making to leave. "The matter is over," he stated, his voice low, calm, bored. "You have been informed of where the diocese stands on the matter. Thank yourself that you still have a church to be repaired." He motioned with his head that Pince-nez should also stand. The other man did so, not once taking his eyes off the glowering ball of hate on the other side of the desk. "You are to find a contractor to undertake the work for you. A local one would be good; it would show your personal support for the community — something that has come to our attention as lacking during your incumbency. Raise finance from those amongst you who would see themselves as patrons of the Church." Then he turned to leave.

Finally, the fire that burnt inside my employer erupted as he exploded upwards from his chair and slammed his palms down on his fine desk. "This is an outrage! I will take the matter further!"

"Don't bother," called the senior cleric over his shoulder as he and Pince-nez left the room. "Naves are not our responsibility."

Over the next few weeks, I was aware of many heated conversations between my employer and his wife. Well, I say conversations, they were more like one-sided rants from him whilst she just sat and listened: a primly dressed breaker to his relentless waves.

He could not find finance to undertake the work.

He was unable to hire local labour willing to perform the task at the paltry price that his limited funds could spare.

He was losing parishioners in their droves to neighbouring churches and that meant even less income and, as such, a downwards spiral.

I was exceptionally careful when listening to these tirades. I was well aware that eavesdropping would earn me another stint of sleeping outside. On one occasion, I felt a burning sensation in my chest and hurried away before a large coughing fit overcame me. It was a brutal affair and doubled me up. I held my hand across my mouth to try and muffle the sounds for fear of punishment. When the fit subsided and I removed my hand, there was blood in my palm.

I knew that this was not good.

During this period, I saw relatively less of my master as his affairs drew him further away from the parish on fruitless ventures in search of funds to repair his church. This meant that, without her husband to distract her, my mistress decided to lavish unwelcome attention on her humble servant.

"Does that disturb you?" she enquired one day when I was tidying up the vicar's study. I had come across a newspaper which he had discarded upon his desk a few days previous before leaving on business. There, on the front page, was a graphic illustration of another poor unfortunate girl who had met another gruesome fate.

"Has this girl been murdered by the same killer?" I asked, carefully folding the journal to remove the horrid picture from my vision.

Mistress smiled far too unpleasantly. "Why don't you tell me? Read the headline. Inform me as to what the Bare Lane Butcher has been up to this time. It is all very clear therein, I am sure."

"I... I cannot," I blushed.

"Why not? Because you find it distasteful? Like a young lady should?"

I shook my head.

"No. That's not the reason, is it?" She leaned close in to me and snatched the paper from my hands. "It's because you're nothing like a young lady, are you? Your beggar parents never taught you how to read. You're just like this whore," she snapped, slapping me across my startled face with the newspaper. "You're nothing but a gutter snipe. Trash. Effluent. You may fool my husband that you have become polished and trustworthy, but I know you for what you really are. You would have our silver as soon as our backs are turned and be off before we knew.

"But that will never happen. You will never leave."

And with that, she turned and walked out of the study, leaving me shaken, confused and on the verge of tears.

Salvation came for the Vicar in a most unexpected manner.

One morning, as I served him and his wife their usual breakfast, there was a knock at the door. My master shooed me away in order to see who was trying to bother them at this early time of day. I hurried away, ensuring that I looked presentable as I made my way to the front door. I took a breath, turned the handle and pulled the door open. For a moment, there was the most peculiar sensation in my stomach. It was as if I had been grabbed by a giant and turned over on my head. I did not know which way was up and which was down as my ears burst in deafening chords of music.

Then I was aware of a firm hand on my shoulder and a calm voice: "Are you okay, my dear?"

And I was. There was no titan turning my world upside down. There was no sound, the one which would expect to accompany the opening of the tombs of the dead on that last dread day. There was just a man and a youth.

The man was about average height but carried himself as if he were twice the size. He stood erect and confident. His hair was dark and his skin relatively pale. He wore a fashionable dark suit with two curious little lapel pins on one collar. One bore an unusual symbol composed of white lines on a black background and the other seemed to have written upon it a word that I could not read. He also wore dark glasses that covered his eyes from my gaze. Eyes that I instinctively knew would appear much older than his apparent years.

The youth was a lad of a similar age to me. He stood uncomfortably behind his companion, his blue eyes peering out from under a mop of wavy hair that was identical in colour to that of the man.

"I see that your beautiful edifice is in need of repairs," smiled the stranger. "I thought that perhaps I might be able to help."

It took less than three weeks for the repairs to be completed. Almost every skilled labourer and craftsman in the local vicinity found themselves benefiting from the seemingly endless pockets and experience of the parish's mysterious benefactor. I watched as scaffolding was heaved into place to allow workmen to repair the damaged roof. I smelt the scent of freshly carved wood as new pews were installed by numerous gangs of labourers under the watchful eye of a master carver. I smiled as stonemasons realigned newly polished slabs along the length of the nave.

By the end of just over twenty days, it was as if the cataclysm had never occurred.

All except for one thing.

"I am afraid that it is totally beyond repair." The metalworker turned the crushed and split bowl over in his hands as he shrugged his broad shoulders. "It could be patched, but it would most likely find a way to leak."

The dark clad stranger walked up to the west end of the church and stood where the font had once resided. As he did so, I saw a small flagstone rock under his foot and I was sure that it caused him to smile. "Then we shall just have to provide a new one."

"I... I can't begin to thank you," the vicar stuttered. "After all you have provided for us, and at such tremendous speed..."

The benefactor cut him off with a wave of his hand. "Think nothing of it. I told you, this place has special meaning to me. Now," he clasped his hands behind his back and turned to face the amazed onlookers, "I know this little chap just outside of town. I've already taken the liberty of engaging him to fashion us a new font — a stone one this time. I feel though," and I was sure that there was amusement in his voice, although for the life of me I did not know why. It was as if he knew a very old and humorous joke to which only he would understand the punchline. "I feel," he repeated, "that an inscription would be in order. Something relevant." From behind his black lenses, his eyes gripped my employer. "What was it that officious little man said to you about the repairs?"

So it was that, on the following Sunday, just after the first service in the newly refurbished church, I found myself stood at the edge of frame whilst my employer posed proudly in front of his greatest achievement: a new, highly polished, stone font — perfect for cleansing the sins of all those who saw fit to repent under his ministrations.

The unveiling of the font and the recommissioning of the church had drawn quite a crowd. The pews had been packed to their limits with the curious faithful who had come to "Ooo..."

and "Ahhh..." at just how quickly the beautiful work had been completed.

Once the hoi polloi had dispersed, a favoured few remained and preened themselves as a reporter from a national paper, no less, busied himself with arranging the little group as artistically as possible.

I was making to go when the strange benefactor lay a gentle hand on my arm. "Please, my dear, stay."

I glanced nervously at my employer who was holding court with local big wigs and the churchwardens. "I... I... do not feel it would be proper..."

"Oh, I disagree." His voice was low, almost conspiratorial, as he shared a look with his young companion before continuing. "I feel it would be most apt... all things considered."

"Things, sir?" I frowned.

He stroked his smoothly shaven chin. "How might one put it? Let's just say it could be useful for you to be in this photo for future generations." And so it was that I had found myself positioned to the edge of the group.

The camera bulb flashed as the reporter's camera operative snapped us for both the newspaper and for posterity. "You will, of course, be sent a copy of the photo, once it has gone to be sketched for printing," he informed the vicar. Then the photographer cocked his head to one side and frowned. "I must say, that is a most unusual inscription."

"Oh, it's just a little joke," the cleric explained haughtily. "I'm sure you wouldn't understand."

"Okay. But who are the knaves?"

The vicar chuckled and shook his head in a knowing manner. "My dear chap, the nave is what we are stood in right now. This part of the church."

"Yes, I know that. That type of nave is spelt with the letter N. That knave," he pointed at the font, "begins with the letter K. It means: a scoundrel."

I thought the vicar's head was going to snap off as it twisted quickly towards the inscription. Then his jaw fell and he sank onto his knees as his fingers traced the erroneous initial. "No... no... no... It can't be. I didn't look. I was so busy. What will he say?" He clambered up to his feet and scanned the crowd.

The benefactor and the boy were gone.

I couldn't stop myself. The tiniest of laughs escaped my mouth.

The next seven days outside were worth it.

Plus, they were to be the start of my new life.

A.S.Chambers

Daughter

By the time that the vicar and his wife let me back into the house, I could not ignore the looming fact that there was something desperately wrong with me. The week after the installation of the new font was one of the wettest weeks that I had ever known and I had been forced to sleep every night in the drenching precipitation.

To make matters worse, they had not fed me either.

The next Sunday, when his wife came down to point at the back door in order to instruct me to go inside, I was half the girl that I had been seven days previous. I had never been very meaty, and now I could feel every one of my ribs. My wrists looked like they could be snapped in half and used as toothpicks by the smallest of children. Every joint ached within my withered body.

And the cough was worse than ever.

When I finally made it up to my garret, I doubled up in fits of agony as a braying convulsion took control of my weakened form. It was so harsh that I found it impossible to breathe and I succumbed to unconsciousness. Upon waking, I found my cheek stuck to the bare wooden floor by my own dried blood.

I pried myself up and crawled into my tiny bed.

I would not leave it as a human ever again.

I do not know why they left me there in that state. Perhaps they thought it to be more punishment? Perhaps they just wanted me to die quietly before they disposed of me? I know not. What I do recall is that the sun rose and set three times outside my window as I lay immobile in my weakened state. All I could do was watch out the dirty glass as the fiery life-giving ball climbed up into the sky, its rays never even touching me as I lay in shadow, covered in filthy rags, before it fell down past my view, down into darkness. Abandoning me to nightmares of illness and death.

Yet, still I refused to entirely give up.

I could not move, I could barely talk, yet even with my ragged cough and my parched lips, I could still produce the tune that I had heard those weeks previous in the church. I retreated inwards, to escape the painful inevitable and let those three notes echo round the emptiness of my hollow body. They started up in the top of my head where they caressed my synapses, numbing me to the hell in which I lay tormented, then they danced down along my limbs, dulling the pain and the flaring aches, before easing their way into my parched lungs and up my withered oesophagus and out through my drawn, papery lips.

It was a tune so quiet that I was sure no human could hear it.

But someone did hear it, and one night he came to me.

At the time, it all seemed so dreamlike. I am guessing that this was because I was so close to death. One moment, I was alone, a faint whisper of a tune passing my frail lips, the next, there was a tall, blonde man stood next to my bed in the darkness of the room, his massive shoulders blocking out the faint light of the moon.

He bent down low over me and I could see that he was listening carefully to my song, the one that came from my dreams. His eyes were both intent and sad. He ran cold fingers across my cheek and drew a sharp breath.

"Let me take you from this place," he said. "Come with me and you will be strong once more. One with such a beauteous tune inside of them should not be allowed to perish in this hovel."

The corners of my lips managed a weary smile. It would be nice to leave this place. It would be wondrous to walk away from this hellish squalor. "Yes," came the vaguest of susurrations from my dying mouth and he bent down across my neck.

There was no pain.

There was no fear.

The song continued to ring in my ears: the three notes over and over, higher and higher, making me fainter and fainter until there was nothing but bright, white light.

Then there was a deep redness in the light.

It washed into my vision and lapped up against the side of my eyes, staining the pure white. It danced through my head and filled my mouth.

And I drank it down, hungrily.

With each gulp, more and more strength returned to my mummified cadaver. I was aware of atrophied muscles thickening and swelling, brittle bones calcifying and strengthening. My lungs felt as if great weights were removed from their midst.

My eyes opened and I saw the world anew.

That night, I died.

That night, I was reborn.

But first, I had to dream.

After waking from the nightmare that I could not recall, I sat up, slid my legs out of bed and just looked at everything. The whole room around me seemed so different. It was still dark as it was the middle of the night, but everything seemed to shine and glisten to my new eyes. I could see the tiniest motes of dust pirouetting in the moonlight. I reached out and I could feel eddies of a breeze caress my fingertips. I listened and heard a distant owl hooting from what must have been miles away.

Then I inhaled, and I smelt blood.

Rising to my feet, I departed my garret and made my way downstairs, following the sharp, iron aroma. It led me to the bedroom of my employers.

My erstwhile employers.

My saviour stood across the other side of their large wooden bed, looking down at their lifeless forms. They were the palest of pales with precise pairs of puncture wounds adorning their necks.

"There is no redemption for this kind of person," the blonde giant whispered in a voice that only I could possibly hear. "Once you had perished, they would have sought out and destroyed another. They had to be stopped."

I walked around the bed, my eyes not leaving his dark face. I reached up and wiped the spot of blood from his mouth that I had smelt from upstairs. "Is this what we do now?" I asked.

"No," came the reply. "We find the Eternals,

43

protect the Twins, await the Divergence."

"I dreamt. Before. I don't remember..."

"None of us do. But you spoke as you dreamt."

I expected my heart to beat fast. Instead it was inert. "Tell me."

The tall figure gave a heavy sigh and began. "You said you were in a barn. You were not very coherent. You were not alone. There was a man there. He held a gun. He fired."

"Is that how I am to die?"

"Yes. But the gun cannot, will not kill you."

"Why not?"

"You, like me, are now a Child of Cain, a vampire, and we must leave this place immediately."

I nodded and I turned to look at my dead tormentors. There they were, still and recumbent. I felt nothing towards them: no pity, no anger, no remorse. Yet this stranger had shouldered far more emotion than I, and had acted upon it.

Something caught my eye. Something on the nightstand, glossy in the moonlight. I walked over and picked up the small photograph. It showed the font with people stood around it. Living, breathing people. Including a living, breathing me. Carefully, so as not to damage such a precious thing, I held it close to my chest.

I nodded. I was done here.

We left Wellington that night. My father, Doulos, had a carriage waiting for him at a certain place at an allotted time. Apparently, I had not been a planned birth.

"I am still not sure what drew me to you, my child," he explained as we rattled through the night, whilst mortals slumbered cosily in their beds. "I had some mundane business to attend to here this night and I was supposed to be done and away. Then... Then I heard your song.

"I could not ignore it.

"It held me entranced."

I sat quietly, unsure what to say.

"Tell me, child. Where did you learn it?"

I risked a glance up into his dark eyes, framed in contrast against his pale, flawless skin. I saw only curiosity, not the anger that I had been used to over the last few months. Even so, the matter of the song's source still confused me greatly. "It was in a dream," I shrugged. "I do not remember much." My eyes sank back down to studying my hands. Dust from the carriage sparkled delicately around my fingertips, eddying in the movement of the horses and the large wheels.

Doulos said nothing. Instead, he just settled back into his seat and I heard the very sound of his eyelids closing.

The matter was over.

For now.

About an hour before dawn, we arrived at an inn of some sorts. It was far fancier than any that I had ever previously had the misfortune to enter, and I could not help but stare at the fine furnishings with my new eyesight as my father guided me up to our suite of rooms.

"We will rest here during the day," he stated matter-of-factly, as he went around the room, ensuring that the drapes were pulled shut tight. "We will travel onwards tomorrow night."

I nodded obediently, my eyes scanning the room in a nervous fashion.

Doulos frowned. "What is it, my child?"

"Where... where am I to sleep?"

"Oh," a look of shock spread over his face. "Oh, it is not like that. Forgive me. I did not create you to… Oh! No! You are my daughter."

It was then my turn to feel embarrassment. "Oh god, no! That's not what I meant. No, not at all. I did not think…" I shook my head, my cheeks scarlet. "No, I meant…" My voice dropped to a whisper. "Do I have to use a coffin?"

For a moment there was deathly silence as the words sank in, then deep laughter followed as Doulos doubled up in amusement, slapping his thigh in great mirth.

"Gods! I am a poor parent. I lack such paternal grace and enlightenment." He stood, took a breath, then opened a door behind him and showed me through. Inside, stood the grandest bed that I had ever lain eyes upon. "No cheap box for you, my child. No earth from where you were born." There was devilish amusement in his voice. "No. Only the finest mattress, sheets and pillows for you. That is, if you actually need it."

I wandered over to the bed, sat down on the luxurious bedding and raised an eyebrow at him. "What do you mean? Don't our kind sleep during daylight hours?"

My father sighed as he sat down next to me. "Young one, I have so much to teach you. It will take a very long time to learn all the ways of our kind. Perhaps a little at a time?

"Perhaps I can get it right this time?"

I frowned at this, but kept quiet and listened as he continued to speak.

"There are many myths about us. Most are false. Some, unfortunately, are true. Sunlight and flame are deadly to us. We spend the daytime hours in the shadows as best we can. There is no deathly sleep, but you may feel that you wish to nap. Some of our kind can go for years without slumber, others enjoy its embrace. Holy water, garlic, inability to cross running water: absolute poppycock.

"A sharp object through the heart and decapitation will kill us, but then, they would dispatch any mortal too. However, we recover from the gravest of injuries should our heart or head remain intact."

He paused, glanced up at the wall and smiled. "Oh, and one other myth that the storytellers love is also untrue."

He stood, walked over to the wall and lifted down a large, gilt looking glass.

"Here you are," he smiled, turning its mirrored side towards me. "This is what you will be for the rest of your life. Do you like what you see?"

I peered into the oil-lit reflection. My skin shone in the half light and my blue eyes sparkled brilliantly. I ran my fingers through my long, dark, lustrous hair, holding it up behind me as if it were fashioned in a shorter style. Gone was the waif, the orphan, the dying servant girl.

I smiled.

Oh, yes. I liked what I saw.

It was later that day that I found out I was royalty.

Before we left town, Doulos decided that perhaps I ought to have a new wardrobe. He sent for a local tailor to bring some outfits for me to try on. I gasped at all the silks and satins that lay displayed on chairs in our sitting room. Their material rustled delicately in my ears as I ran my fingers across their delightfully smooth material. The garments here were far grander than those that the vicar's wife had ever worn.

She most certainly would not have approved.

I smiled.

I homed in on the simplest of the dresses and held it up against myself. "May I try this one on?" I asked.

Doulos frowned. "Really? It's a tad plain, don't you think? What about this one?" He produced a dress that was bright scarlet and had so many frills that I was not sure where I would be able to clamber inside to don it.

"I... I... don't think it's quite me."

"But the colour would complement your hair."

I shrugged. "People would be looking at me all the time."

"And what is wrong with that?"

"I... I'm not used to it."

"Well, you're going to have to get used to it."

"Really? I'm not sure." I glanced at the tailor, unsure what to say in front of him.

Doulos recognised my hesitation. "Good man, perhaps you could give us half an hour or so?" He handed him some coins. "I believe the ale downstairs is very fine." Then, when the retailer had left, my father turned to me and dropped the bombshell as to why I would be the centre of attention, at least in the vampire world.

"You're their king?" I gasped.

He nodded.

I slumped down into the nearest armchair. Not only had I been raised from mortality to the life supernatural, but apparently I had now been birthed into royalty.

"So does that make me a princess?"

"I guess so, technically."

"Am I your heir?"

Doulos' face fell.

"What's the matter?"

He came and sat next to me, laying his cold hand on mine. "Daughter, before I came to you, I had been abroad for a while, in the Americas. While I was there, I came across a young man who was in a similar state to you. He was dying from very grievous wounds. He had no one. His family had been butchered.

"I made him my son.

"He is your brother."

It appeared that my family was growing by the minute. "What is his name?"

"He took the name Justice."

"Took?"

"When our kind are born to our new life, we leave our old one behind us. To illustrate the fact, we adopt a new name. I took Doulos because I had been a slave."

I frowned at him. "I didn't know that there were white slaves anymore."

"There were when I was born."

My mouth opened and words tried to tumble out as realisation hit.

"I am almost two thousand years old," he smiled.

"But... but you just said that you've only now made children. Have you been alone all that time?"

"Not all of it. At first, I was accompanying my mother, the then queen. Then, when she passed, I spent time with others of our kind around the world. I just never felt the need to create progeny. Until now, that is. I find the whole concept quite confusing. I am somewhat at sea with the whole matter."

"Is Justice with others of our kind?"

Doulos was silent.

"Father!" I gasped. "You mean to say that you left him on his own?"

Still the king said nothing.

I however, did not hold back. I stood and poured word after word onto his bowed head. I scolded him for abandoning his firstborn in such a wild and savage country. I tutted and tisked as I strutted around the room, rambling on about how the poor mite would have no one to talk to, no one to share his problems with.

"We must do something about it," I finally announced, marching into my room with the most practical outfit that had been brought for me to try on.

"What is there that I can do?" Doulos wailed.

I bustled back into the living room, dressed in a fine travelling suit. "We can go across to America and find him.

"Now."

I suppose, in my young, romantic mind, I saw us instantly dashing to the nearest port, grabbing a ship and heading straight over to the land of the Wild West before tracking down my lost elder sibling.

The reality was somewhat more mundane as our passage had to be properly arranged.

However, it did mean that I got to meet some more of our kind: one of whom I would be spending considerable time with later on in my life.

"Well, isn't she a darling!"

"Such a pretty little thing!"

"I always knew he would make a child."

"Needs fattening up a bit, mind..."

Ah, yes. He had been right. I was very much the centre of attention when Doulos' subjects found out about me. I was cooed over, examined, poked, prodded and advised, advised, advised more than I had ever been in my mortal life.

I took it all with good grace and a smile. I decided that I couldn't really blame them; it wasn't every day that their king produced a progeny.

However, it started to wear thin somewhat, so after about the third night of full on attention, I managed to back inconspicuously out of a small door and find solitude in a small garden in the town house where we were currently lodging. I wandered out into the cool night air and breathed deep the scent of flowers, the names of which I was completely ignorant, being a town girl. They were big and full, their pink petals emitting a powerful and intoxicatingly fresh scent. I closed my eyes and let the perfume wash over me. As I did so, I felt myself truly relax for the first time since I had been made a vampire. As my muscles softened and my head cleared, I became aware of the old three notes rising and falling inside me and I opened my mouth to give them voice. It was a soft song, a gentle lullaby for the flowers around me, not some powerful cataclysmic anthem wrapped up in the devastation of a church. As I sang, I swayed softly and imagined that I was free in the night, the scent of the flowers my companion. Under the moonlight, I serenaded the things of beauty and they, in turn, rewarded me with their aromatic scent.

"I can see why our king was transfixed by your song."

A tall figure stepped out of the shadows and my tune stuttered to a halt.

"Oh, I'm terribly sorry. I didn't mean to startle you. Your song was truly beautiful." The male vampire came into the light of the moon and I looked up into the face of the one who would become my closest friend. "Look at me. Where are my manners? My name is Marcus." He gave a polite bow.

"I'm Esther," I replied.

His grey moustache twitched. "I thought that was your human name?"

"I haven't chosen a new one yet." I sat down in a wicker chair next to the flowers. "I find it rather daunting. Imagine being saddled with a name for eternity that you realise somewhere down the line that you hate!"

A wry smile touched the lips that rested beneath his neatly groomed moustache. "Indeed. That would be quite hellish. I'm just glad that I was a fan of Roman philosophy when I was human."

My puzzled look encouraged him to continue.

"Marcus Aurelius was both a man of knowledge and an Emperor of Rome. He was one of the wiser ones amongst a ramshackle bunch of power-crazed lunatics."

I sighed. "You sound so confident. It must be so much easier for you."

"How come?"

"Being a vampire for so long."

"Oh yes, a dreadfully long time." His eyes twinkled in the moonlight.

I frowned. "What do you mean?"

"Looks can be deceptive, my dear. Just because I appear older than you physically, doesn't make me an older Child of Cain. I am but a week old. I'm actually rather pleased that you came along. It's sort of taken the pressure off me. My mother was quite bursting with pride at my creation."

We both chuckled.

"I have a lot to learn," I conceded.

"As do I. Perhaps we will learn things together?"

I shook my head. "Doulos and I sail to America in a few days' time."

"Ah, to track down your sibling."

I nodded.

"Well then," he slapped his palms on his knees. "You will most definitely need a new name before you go. I'm quite sure you won't have time to think of one whilst you're dashing around playing Cowboys and Indians. What's worse, you need something suitable. Heaven forbid you come back with a Western name!" The word dripped with exaggerated contempt. "We can't have a princess called Cactus or Red Eye now, can we?"

I laughed and Marcus smiled.

"I'm sorry, I just don't have a clue."

I caught him studying me intently.

"What is it?"

"I would have thought it was obvious," he shrugged. "Here you are, the girl that drew a king to her presence by her song that echoed through the night. Our monarch has apparently always been a somewhat dour sort, yet you have rejuvenated him and given him life.

"I think, perhaps, you should call yourself Nightingale."

Nightingale.

I heard the name resonate around inside my head, the song rising to caress it, to lift it up into the night.

Nightingale.

I had a name.

Sister

"He's this way."

We were running across what, to me, looked for all intents and purposes like a barren landscape. The ground around us was desiccated and arid. Where once there had been grassland, now there was just dry, ugly scrub. Previously, majestic buffalo had roamed over these plains, tracked and hunted by an indigenous population, but European farming methods had reduced the ground to ruin.

Just like its peoples.

We had arrived on the East coast at a thriving city. There had been no time for me to stop and marvel at the modern buildings that were seeming to spiral up out of the earth in an attempt to conquer the sky above. Instead, Doulos had ushered me onto an enormous behemoth of a steam train that had forged a path for us out of civilisation and into this godforsaken wilderness.

Once we had reached the outlying towns, we had progressed on foot. We could have taken a carriage, but Doulos reasoned that it would have been restrictive.

Besides, we were far swifter than the most athletic stallion.

So we had travelled from town to town, gleaning bits and pieces of scant tales: stories of a tall, silent stranger who would pass through as if on a mysterious mission that he shared with no one. He kept himself to himself, shunned the company of others and made no trouble.

That was, until he had reached an old mining town called Salem.

There he had made quite the impression.

He had apparently also picked up a companion: a young orphan boy.

Like father, like son? I had wondered.

There had been carnage. Justice had single-handedly taken down the corrupt, bullying sheriff and his cronies. Doulos and I had visited the scene of the gunfight and it had been there that I had first heard the word that made Children of Cain feel sick to the stomach.

Construct.

The sheriff, Carson, had not been human. He had been made of clay, fashioned by the hand of some unknown power. A being that wanted to bring about one thing: the Divergence.

"How did Justice kill it?" I had asked.

"Why do you think we have fangs?" came the sardonic reply.

As we continued our journey, my father and king filled me in some more on our nemeses. Their creation was veiled in mystery. All that we could glean was that somewhere in the future someone was amassing a vast army of them and systematically sending them back in history to wipe us out.

This was a task in which they were ruthlessly efficient.

They may look like humans and walk like humans, but they possess a deadly surprise up their sleeve: they have the ability to change shape. Their viscous structure means that they can turn body parts into projecting weapons such as a lance or a knife. Many Children of Cain have met their demise at the end of such a projectile.

They can be defeated, though. Draining them of their life fluid is the usual, preferred method. Sometimes they can be slowed down first, via decapitation or dismemberment, but they have to be finished off in order to ensure that they do not rise again. Fire, as against us, is also a useful tool. Being made from clay, intense heat kills them, baking them hard like a statue.

"The eruption at Pompeii did us a great service," Doulos had mused.

There is, however, one property of constructs which aids us immensely.

They smell wrong.

Like a boot that has been left to moulder in a foetid swamp, their body odour is gut-wrenchingly distinctive. Those of them who know what they are often try to conceal this aroma with perfumes or strong scents. But those who have not yet awoken to their true nature, are easier to track down and pick off before they are activated.

As soon as we had entered our current town, Doulos had picked up two distinct scents: that of his son and that of clay-based trouble.

"I don't think he's with the constructs." We had slowed down to a more mortal-like speed — better not to spook the locals — and my father was busy gathering intelligence from the air around us. "No. They are away from him at the moment." He paused, concern wrinkling his brow and he looked me square in the face. "I should track my son, but we cannot ignore their threat. Can you follow them? Observe them?"

I smiled back at him. "I'll give it my best. They'll never know I'm there."

My father frowned. "All the same, you are young, inexperienced. I have not taught you how to hunt yet. Should they sense you and attack..."

I drew my lips back and pointed to my sharp incisors. "Can't be that hard, can it? I latch on, bite hard, then suck."

"Sometimes they are tricky." He slung his pack down off his shoulder and reached inside, pulling out a long object wrapped in a dark cloth. "I think, perhaps, you ought to take this as insurance. It served me well when I was younger." A wry smile touched his old lips. "I would appreciate it back in one piece."

I pulled the fabric away and drew a highly polished sword from its scabbard. My face stared back at me from the shining surface of its wickedly sharp blade. "So, if they spot me, a quick slice with this should slow them down?"

Doulos' smile faded. He nodded slowly, made to leave, then stopped to turn to me once more. "Please take care, my child."

"I fully intend to," I smiled.

He hesitated momentarily before nodding once more and heading off in the opposite direction.

Once he was out of sight, I slipped the blade back into its sheath before doubling over and fighting off crippling nausea.

What the hell was I thinking?

I was just a few weeks old and here I was, volunteering to take out an unknown number of shapeshifting death machines?

I pulled myself up, took a deep breath, almost

gagged again, then set off in pursuit of the noxious odour.

I could do this.

I could do this!

Father had only instructed me to observe them, that was all. The sword... Well, that and a pointy set of teeth were just a last resort. Weren't they? It wasn't as if I would have to confront these things, was it?

Just observe.

Yes, just observe.

My stomach cramped a sarcastic retort.

Since when was anything ever that simple?

I was supposed to have been the daughter of loving parents. They had died.

I was supposed to have cared for my brother. He had died.

I was supposed to have been a maid for a respected member of the clergy. He had abused me and died.

There was a pattern forming here. I didn't like it. Was I a Jonah? Was I doomed to live my life in the belly of the beast while all around me perished?

I pressed the reassuring weight of the blade against my hip as I made my way through the sprawling streets. This was not the time for such thoughts. Judging by the lethal nature of the constructs as Doulos had described them, I needed my mind to be very firmly in the here and now rather than wandering the darkened alleys of existential doubt.

To ground myself back in the task at hand, I took a tentative sniff of air. They were close. Very close. The town reeked of horse excrement, soot, alcohol and the great unwashed, but under all those mundane aromas there was still the distinct tang of something that felt incredibly wrong.

I slowed my pace as I walked through the near empty streets. My eyes caught sight of movement down the far end of the road, near a side alley. My ears caught a hint of words on the still night air.

I sighed, steadied myself and made for the creatures that could impale me in the blink of an eye.

As I drew nearer, there was the definite sound of chatter. It sounded so human.

It also sounded elderly.

I frowned as I made out snippets of talk in a female voice about the doings of the day just gone and how the price of vegetables had recently risen. A male voice snapped a response, saying that such things were silly and pointless. There were far more important matters to worry about.

I nodded. Yes. This would be the tell-tale sign. A clue to their monstrous makeup.

"I mean," he continued, "what if they continue to expand the railway in the way that they do? What effect do you think it will have on the local area? All those new ruffians from the east coming here?"

Seriously? Constructs worried about politics and migration? I inhaled as I drew nearer to the alley. The same aroma churned my guts. There was no one else on the street. It had to be them. But they just didn't sound hideous.

I rounded the corner of the alley, keeping to the dark of the shadows and caught my first glimpse of them. They were, as my ears had informed me, an elderly couple. They looked like they were both in their sixties, at least. The woman was now haranguing the man about fussing over things that were inevitable and what business of theirs was it, anyway? The chap just shrugged his bent shoulders and surrendered to what looked like the usual matrimonial status quo.

Was I missing something here?

Still, there was the godawful smell.

And, came a little voice from the back of my head, what are an elderly couple doing in a darkened alley in the middle of the night?

It was then that I heard the man say, "Hello sonny."

I drew closer, desperate not to draw attention to myself. The two figures were stood at a bend in the alley. I reached out with my senses and immediately picked up a third scent — a definitely human scent.

I wanted to get closer to see who this newcomer was, but to do so would definitely reveal my location to my quarries. Instead, I reached out with my ears, focussing my senses on what lay around the bend in the alley.

A heartbeat.

A fast one.

A young one.

Sonny.

Justice was travelling with a young boy.

Surely not? That would be one hell of a coincidence.

The seemingly elderly couple entered the section of the alley around the corner, passing out of sight. I used this moment to draw closer, still listening.

"I'm just collecting my thoughts." Yes. It was a young boy.

"In an alley," the old man chuckled. "Surely that's not a good idea? There could be all sorts about." The emphasis on the words froze my spine and the aroma of construct flared more intensely in my nostrils. This was not good. Most definitely not good.

But what was I to do?

"I'll be fine," the young lad assured the monsters made from clay. "I have a protector."

As if to reaffirm my previous thought, the construct said, "Funny, but I don't see the vampire anywhere near right now."

I actually heard the boy's heart skip a literal beat as realisation dawned. He knew what these creatures were now. My brother had obviously warned him. I remained as one with the shadows and rounded up behind the creatures. The boy slipped down off a crate upon which he had been seated. There was no mistaking the look of fear from the whites of his eyes that contrasted the enveloping gloom around him. "What did you say?" His voice was dry, parched, terrified.

Then came the noise that I have heard far too many times since and has always been the herald to sadness and pain. It was wet and elastic, like a potter dropping his clay on the floor, ruining what should have been a thing of beauty but instead creating something awful upon which to gaze — a mutilated abhorrence.

I drew the blade and acted without thought.

I acted purely on instinct.

I acted as a Child of Cain, a vampire.

The male was the first. He had advanced closest to the boy, so proved to be the most imminent threat. There was next to no resistance as the keenly edged sword hacked him in twain from shoulder to waist. His severed body parts slouched to the floor, wet ooze seeping from the smooth wounds.

The next was the female. She, I dispatched in the more traditional way. Only partially transformed, I grabbed her by the neck, catching just a glint of terror in her eyes before plunging my teeth deep into her neck. The sensation as I drank was like nothing I had ever experienced. As I gulped down deep draughts of her life liquid, my veins and arteries opened to the welcome feast. There was the sensation of light-headedness and exhilaration as chemicals hit my brain and my nervous system. I imbibed faster, draining every drop of fluid from her withering corpse until she was nothing but dust, both in my hands and down the front of my finely fashioned garments.

I stood back, staring in awe at what I had done, what I had been born to do and, as the world around me started to edge back into focus, I was aware of a familiar scent joining me in the alley. It was my father. I turned to see him finishing off the remains of the male, making sure that it would never rise again.

Then there was another presence, a blur, and the boy was being lifted into the arms of a man taller than me but shorter than my father. He was broad of shoulder and ruggedly handsome of face. His grey eyes scanned the boy for any signs of misdeed then, when satisfied, they turned to us and widened before he sank reverentially to one knee in front of Doulos.

"Your majesty," came the deep, western accent.

Doulos, approached the vampire and lifted him, gently to his feet. "My son and heir," he whispered. "Let me introduce you to your sister."

I could not help but smile at my brother's dumbfounded confusion, and I stuck out my hand in greeting. "Hello. My name is Nightingale."

The events of the next twenty-four hours still haunt me.

They started off as joyous emotions of

discovery, wonder and beauty.

They finished as tragedy, death and betrayal.

I went from the blissful existence of being a daughter, a sister, a princess to the haunted desolation of one who has been orphaned, been abandoned, has had unwanted responsibility thrust into their trembling hands.

When I met my brother, Justice, in the back alley of a small western settlement, the name of which I cannot even recall, I had no way of knowing that my life would be even more radically altered than when I had been made a vampire, just a few weeks previous.

It all began so well.

It all began so joyous.

This was because of the boy.

He was a sweet little lad of about ten or so. He was thin, malnourished and could probably be knocked over if you so much as breathed on him. However, his eyes were full of wonder. He adored my quiet sibling and followed him everywhere like the sweetest little puppy. So close was he on Justice's heels that I expected my brother to trip over him every time he turned to speak to our father.

And a lot to talk about they had.

We retired, before sunrise, to a suitable hostel and my father and brother immediately settled down into a deep, quiet parley. It felt quite peculiar, not being the centre of Doulos' attention. Since my birth, there had just been the two of us in our little family. The dynamic was now completely different as our group had instantly doubled. So, I guess it was only natural that I should gravitate towards the boy. I ordered some supper to be sent up and gave him plenty to eat before he settled down to slumber during the daylight hours.

He awoke just as the sun set once more and freshened himself with water from the pitcher by our china washbasin. His eyes began to wander around the room, as those of children are wont to do, trying to find something to amuse himself with as his guardian and his guardian's father continued to converse.

Eventually, I noticed that his eyes had begun to inspect me, or rather my attire.

"You like my clothes?"

His pale cheeks flushed a bright crimson and I couldn't help but laugh.

"It's okay to look," I reassured him. "I'm guessing it's not like you've seen anything quite like us before? Well, apart from," I cast an eye at Justice, talking intently to our father, "my rather dour older brother there."

The boy's eyes followed mine. "About that..."

I poked at the hearth to raise some more flames out of the burning logs. He looked like he could use the heat, poor mite. "What?"

The boy shuffled slightly in his seat. "You say that he's your brother, yet you don't look similar at all. You're all, you know, pretty," he blushed even more, "and he's so... so..."

"Serious?" I volunteered in hushed conspiratorial tones.

The boy's head bobbed up and down.

Well, he was certainly right about that one. I didn't think that I had seen Justice crack a single smile since our meeting. My lips turned up at the edge, spread into a grin, then developed into a light chuckle. "We're not kin like humans are," I explained. "We just share the same father. He... created us."

The boy's eyes wandered back to the two male vampires. This time I could see them studying

Doulos. They tracked the length of his mane of blonde hair, took in his fine clothing that hinted at a physique of athletic perfection and marvelled at just how damned tall he was. But most of all, they stared in awe at his total presence.

"And he is your king?"

"That he is."

"So, does that make you a princess?"

"I guess it does," I smiled. "I guess it does."

My eyes followed his and regarded my father, my king. There he sat, deep in conversation, the ruler of an entire species. His fine clothes were tailored to fit perfectly, as were mine.

Then I looked at the boy next to me and the rags that were barely holding themselves together: seams popped, cuffs ragged. I ran my fingers over his shirt and the grimy fabric felt stiff to the touch. "How long have you had this?"

He shrugged. "A while, I guess. I haven't gotten any new clothes since my pa died."

The poor little mite! I reached out and stroked his cheek. "Well, I think it's about time that you did. Come on."

I stood and crossed the room to the door, beckoning him to follow. "We're just going shopping," I threw over my shoulder to my father and my brother. "Won't be long."

Oh, that I had kept the child in his rags!

It was early evening as we made our way down the dusty street. The sun had set and the moon was creeping up over the horizon. There was a chill in the air but neither that nor the coldness of my skin could temper the emotional warmth that I felt spreading through my soul.

I had a family again!

I had a father, a brother and a nephew (of

sorts).

Okay, so it was not your traditional family set up, but it was certainly more than I had experienced since my human family had died, one by one.

I was going to make the most of it.

"I think," I said as we approached the local tailor's store, "that we will need to find you something fashionable as well as practical, don't you agree?"

The boy looked me up and down. "Will it be colourful, like yours?"

"We shall have to see what they have in stock," I shrugged. "I don't think Doulos will want us to stay here too long, so there won't be time to have anything made to measure."

My little companion grinned. "That sounds fine." Then he hesitated as we walked up to the wooden door. "Will it be expensive?"

"I'm sure I will be able to afford something for you," I winked. "Oh!"

"What is it?"

I frowned at the closed sign that hung in the window. "It appears we are somewhat late. Just a minute." I rapped on the glass with my knuckles. There was no immediate reply, so I repeated the action, which was rewarded by the sight of an elderly man peering through the dusty glass.

"Hello!" I beamed in as friendly manner as possible. "Sorry to disturb you, but we're passing through and my young companion here needs new clothes."

The man frowned and eyed us with apparent suspicion. "It's late. I'm closed."

"I know. I'm really sorry, but we couldn't get here earlier." I fished into my jacket and produced a leather pouch that was obviously full of money. "I'm happy to pay that bit extra for the inconvenience."

His eyes held mine, looked at the boy then practically goggled at the bag.

An hour later and there were discarded clothes strewn around the small shop.

"There's so much choice," the boy sighed. "I... I just don't know what to choose."

I passed him a smooth, beautifully woven cotton shirt. "Well, which do you like the most?"

"I'm not sure..."

A laugh escaped my mouth and I looked around the varying piles of jackets, shirts, pants and accessories. "Well, obviously you need a number of shirts and a couple of pairs of pants."

He nodded.

"So..." I picked up the items that he had spent the longest trying on, quite obviously enjoying the luxurious feel of the rich materials, to which his grubby fingers were unaccustomed. "Shall we assume that these are suitable?"

He nodded with more vigour and I passed the clothes to the shopkeeper.

"Now, what about a jacket?"

His eyes strayed to a velvet coat that hung on the back of a nearby chair. He had tried it on first of all, running his fingers through the lush material.

"So, what about this, then?"

"It was expensive," he whispered.

"So it'll last a long time." I picked it up and helped him into the heavy piece of clothing. His young face immediately radiated joy as his fingers went back to idly drawing pictures and lines in the soft material. He was quite clearly smitten.

"Well? What about it?"

He nodded exuberantly.

I grinned and, for a moment, I saw a younger me stood there, existing in an alternate life — one without death and poverty.

"I think we have a winner!"

The shopkeeper asked if we wanted the jacket wrapping up with the shirts and the pants.

I watched fondly as the youngster was lost in his own world, just enjoying the moment. "I don't think we could part him from it if we tried."

The elderly man smiled at this, then grinned even more when I paid him far over the asking price. He had been terribly attentive and deserved the financial reward for opening up at such a late hour.

We left and headed back up the street towards where we were lodged.

I was relaxed, happy and chatting idly to the boy.

In short, my guard was down.

I'm not sure how, but as we talked, our conversation manoeuvred itself onto the topic of my second birth. Onto the night that Doulos became my father.

"How did he find you?"

The innocent eyes gazed up at me. It was a natural question. His new father, my brother, had found him, taken him away to a new and wondrous life. He wanted to know how I had come to mine.

My mind drifted back to my dark, mouldering attic, to a shadowy room that had been abandoned by the sun. In the back of my head, three notes that I had not heard for many weeks susurrated their repetitive song.

I gave the boy a somewhat abridged version. I informed him that I had been ill, that there had been nightmares and that I had sung to keep my spirits up. I told him that the song had been what had drawn Doulos to me.

I did not mention the two bodies that had been left drained downstairs.

"Doulos saved me," I finished.

It was finally, at that moment, that I realised we were not alone. I spun around to see three rough sorts standing behind us, spread across an otherwise deserted side street.

"There's no one here to save you now, my pretty." The deliberate manner in which the words were delivered and the overwhelming aroma of cheap bourbon both reassured me that these men were no real threat, but also caused me to worry just in case they tried something stupid. "Now, why don't you just hand over those fine garments and some of your gold, then we'll be on our way."

I eased the boy behind me, standing as a shield between him and an unwanted incident. "You don't want to do this," I tried to keep my voice low, unthreatening but also in control of a potentially volatile situation.

The leader of the three was undeterred. "Really?" His pockmarked cheeks stretched into a gruesome leer as his eyes rose and fell the length of my body. "Oh, but I think we do. You come into our town dressed in your fancy clothes, ordering our shopkeepers around and don't think that you'll have to pay for the privilege? Now hand the goods over!"

"No," I refused, an edge sharpening my reply. "We're leaving now." I turned my back to them, placed a hand on my ward and made to walk away.

It was when one of the thugs made to grab the boy that things went to hell in a handbag. I was more aware of his agonised screaming than I was of my instinct to grab his offending limb and snap it next to the elbow. As he lay howling in the filth that clogged the gutter, the inevitable happened: his comrades drew their weapons.

I did likewise.

I couldn't stop myself. I knew there would be repercussions but the look of fear on their face at the sight of my sharpened incisors made it almost worthwhile.

"Leave us!" I spat at our attackers and they scrambled off into the night.

"Oh, we are in such big trouble," I moaned.

At first, I thought that there would just be a scolding from my father, my king, then we would have to hastily leave town before dawn to ensure that we were forgotten.

What's that you say? A pretty young girl, you saw? With fangs, you say? Can't see her around now, can we? How much did you say you'd drunk?

I guess that I was still a complete innocent when it came to folk harbouring a grudge.

We had tried to take a more circuitous route back to our lodgings, just in case trouble had tried to follow us. This caution had proven worthwhile when we heard the shout of, "There they are!" hurled at us down one more horse shit-smelling street that had looked just like so many others in this godforsaken place.

This time, there were more than three. A lot more.

The rabble was armed with guns, knives and varying instruments designed to cause as much pain as possible to those that they feared and did not understand.

If it had just been me, I could have made myself instantly scarce: nip around a corner, jump up onto a roof and nimbly make my way across town in the dark, whilst avoiding further confrontation.

However, my companion was not so able, being a mere mortal.

I chivvied him along as fast as I could: me trying to stay slow, him desperate to keep up. At one point, he tripped. I caught him before he could cause himself mischief, but his parcel of clothes fell out of his outstretched arms and bounced off into the mud. He reached out to grab them.

"Leave them," I whispered. "We can buy more." Then I whisked him away, down towards a side alley. "Quick, down here." I rushed him as fast as his legs could carry him and located a suitable hiding place. There were some old barrels stacked in a haphazard fashion towards the end of the ginnel. They stank of something rank, but they would do.

They would have to do.

I pulled him in close to me and covered him from sight. As I did, I felt his small body quaking against my side. He was utterly terrified.

This was all my fault, but I would sort it. All we had to do was stay here, quiet, out of the way until the horde passed by. Once the wick of their fervour had burnt down, they would meander off to their homes or to a tavern and forget all about us.

That was the plan.

It was a poor plan.

"We saw them come down here!"

I cursed under my breath.

"Split up and search the alleys!"

The boy whimpered into my breast.

What to do? What to do?

They were just seconds away from locating us and there were far too many of them. A handful of rednecks I could easily fight off, but a few dozen?

We needed a diversion.

I drew back from the trembling youngster and looked him hard in his wide, open eyes. "Whatever you do," I instructed him, "do not leave this place. Stay here and you will be safe. I will lead them away and come back for you."

There was no reply, no response whatsoever from the boy. Fear had him completely in its vice-like grip.

I heard the heavy tread of a determined footstep entering the mouth of our alley.

"Please. Just nod. Anything. Tell me you understand."

The boy curled up in a ball behind the barrel.

My heart curled up in worry.

That would just have to do. There was no more time.

I drew myself up and erupted out of the alley, shrieking like a banshee, causing all around to focus their attention on me. There were shouts and curses as I knocked some of our pursuers over as if they were skittles, but I could not afford to look back. I could not give the slightest inclination that I had left a defenceless young boy knotted up in petrified terror at the end of the alley.

There was the unmistakable sound of hurried footsteps clattering after me.

I allowed myself a satisfied smile.

Foolish girl.

Foolish, foolish girl.

I decided to circle back to the alley after about fifteen minutes or so. I was satisfied that I had led the rampaging horde a merry dance around their pathetic little town. Feeling quite satisfied with myself, I dropped down from the roof of a stable and brushed my clothes down. Wellington had not been the cleanest of places, but it had never been dusty.

Wellington.

A curious feeling crept into my heart. Longing.

I had endured a hellish time there, abused by my employers and made to act as a second or third class citizen, yet there was part of me that longed to go back there, to the church.

To the font.

Over the silence of the night, three repetitive notes drifted back into my subconscious.

Shaking my head, I banished them far away. This was no time for distractions. I had to go and collect the boy from his hiding place.

Carefully, just in case any hoodlums still lurked in the nearby vicinity, I made my way back into the street off which the alley spurred. At once, familiar voices reached my ears and my smile broadened as I fell in step behind my brother.

"Greetings sister," came the deep American drawl. He didn't even need to look around to know that I was there.

"Greetings brother."

Justice turned and cast a slow eye over my clothing. "You seem somewhat dishevelled."

I noticed that Doulos had made his way into the alley, obviously to fetch the young lad. "Oh, you know. A late night run and all that."

There was no reply from my brother and my smile suddenly felt somewhat nervous.

"Let's get your ward and leave this place, shall we?"

"Agreed."

We walked after our father into the foul-smelling alley and I immediately experienced two dreadful sensations.

The first was of mental confusion. Doulos was stood there, alone. He was on his own, by the barrels. Where I had left the boy. But the boy was not there. Doulos was on his own. This wasn't right at all. He couldn't be alone. I had left the boy there…

The second was of physical disorientation. My feet flew up off the floor and a wall was slamming against my back. A hand was clenched around my throat and harsh words were being shouted at me. There was the presence of someone very close: extremely close. They were angry, furious. Over and over, they were pounding me into the wall and pieces of wood were splintering from the building, digging into my back. All the time there was the thump, thump, thump of me hitting an immovable object time and time again, my feet dangling in the air as if I was levitating off the floor.

Then there was freedom and I was falling down to the ground, smacking it hard with my knees and the palms of my hands. I was shaking my head, desperate to try and clear my head, to make sense of what had just happened.

I turned my aching neck and saw an incredible sight. Doulos had grabbed his irate son by the back of his long overcoat and was holding him out at arm's length as the younger vampire kicked and flailed, cursing me and screaming for my blood.

The boy was gone.

It was my fault.

I felt a tear track down my cheek. Wiping it away, I stared in fascination at its scarlet sheen before my tired voice managed the only words that I could say at that moment in time. "I'm sorry. I'm so sorry."

This poor man had watched powerless as his first family had been brutally murdered, then his father had abandoned him and now his sister had lost him the closest thing he had to a replacement son.

His reaction was totally understandable.

After a while, the tempest eased and Justice began to calm down. Doulos dropped him in an unceremonial fashion to the litter-strewn floor before replacing his hat and dusting off his frock coat. His eyes burned down at his errant children. "Enough of this!" he demanded. "What's done is done. We must leave."

Justice and I stood and steadied ourselves. The creature that now stalked away towards the exit of the alley was our father, our king. He was two millennia old and had a wisdom that was far greater than our combined knowledge which was more akin to the presence of mind of an ant. Should he wish, he could turn, strike us down, rip out our hearts and dispatch us there and then.

He was not to be trifled with.

"No," said my brother.

"No," said I.

Doulos paused mid-stride. He did not even bother to face us. This was a forgone decision. His mind was made up. We were to do as he said. "We cannot stay here. Enough damage has been done. We cannot save the boy without revealing ourselves. We must leave. Now."

As one, Justice and I sped past him at supernatural speed, leaving his demands to echo around an empty alleyway.

"Plan?"

"Grab the boy. Leave."

"That simple?"

"That simple."

I rolled over onto my side and studied the face of my sibling. He was like a stone grotesque peering out over the scene below. "What if anyone tries to stop us?"

Justice said nothing. He just continued to stare down at the crowd in the square. I could see no movement in his features. Gone was the anger. Instead there was just calm, calculated observation.

He looked exactly like a predator hiding in the grass, calculating the quickest, deadliest way to bring down its kill. There was no passion, no emotion, no hint of any future guilt. There was a job to do and it would be enacted in an exact manner. A ruthless manner.

I looked back out at the crowd. They were standing expectantly outside the town hall, observers who had dragged themselves out of their beds to see just what all the ruckus was.

How many of these were actually part of the mob that had grabbed the boy?

How many were just innocent bystanders?

How many were going to end up as collateral damage when the tempest broke above them?

I couldn't let my brother off the leash. We had to enact this rescue in a controlled manner.

"Well?" I pressed.

"We concentrate on saving the boy then deal with anyone who gets in our way."

I shifted my gaze back to the killing machine next to me. Still there was nothing. What the hell was he planning? Go in with all guns blazing, teeth slashing?

"No one gets hurt," I insisted. "Promise."

His head finally moved, swivelling on his neck so that his eyes fixed on me. And there was the anger. "If anyone gets hurt, it's your fault for not protecting the boy."

My stomach lurched as his punch hit true, but I couldn't just lie here and take it. "Oh, don't you go pinning this on me!" I hissed. "And why do you just call him the boy? Why don't you use his name?"

Justice snapped his face forward once more and my question slammed up against a wall of silence.

My mouth hung open in disbelief. "You are joking, aren't you? You don't know his name?"

Justice pulled out one of his six-shooters and silently inspected the barrel of the weapon.

"Unbelievable!" I continued to berate him in a stage whisper that couldn't be heard down below. "You drag him away from his normal life into ours, where the monsters under the bed are real, and you don't even bother to find out his name?"

"So," Justice said, still studiously inspecting his gun, "what is it then?"

My stomach lurched once more and I felt instantly nauseous. My accusations were suddenly as barren as the dusty plains which surrounded this tin pot little town.

"Perhaps you asked him when you treated him like a doll, when you were dressing him up in fine clothes? Perhaps you enquired when he sat scared in the depths of a shit-smelling alleyway?"

I could not manage any words, any smart come back. I felt too sick to open my mouth. All I could do was lie there, atop a dust-battered roof and glower at my older sibling.

My older sibling who had hit the nail exactly on the head. Not once had I asked the boy his name. Not once. Why ever not? Surely it's the first thing you do when you meet someone: you introduce yourself and then enquire as to what they, themselves, are called. Sure, you may forget their name as time passes, but you always make the effort to be friendly, to be civil.

It's human nature.

But then, I was no longer human.

"I thought not," he continued, snapping open the six-shooter and counting the bullets within. "Names are funny things to our kind, aren't they? They portray what we represent rather than who we actually are. Is it so strange that neither of us thought to enquire of his?"

With that, he leapt down into the street, guns drawn.

All I could do was watch the shooting match, and I hated to admit it, but I was seriously impressed. There were no fatal shots. One took out the kneecap of an idiot who actually dared to raise his shotgun at the force of nature that stormed its way through the crowd. The second blasted a wrist of someone who screamed as his pistol fell to the floor. Finally, Justice shot one round up into the night air. This one caused the rest of the crown to scatter, now convinced that they definitely had somewhere better to be.

I took this as my cue. I dropped lightly down into the square and walked up to my brother who was now stood by the door of the town hall. His ear was pressed against the solid wood as his hands automatically reloaded the spent bullets. "I count twelve heartbeats, one racing almost twice as fast as the others," he stated. I was about to ask him what we were going to do next, when he raised his foot and pounded it against the door. It flew clean off its hinges and exploded into the building. This immediately incapacitated the two guards that had been posted by the entrance in order to stop anyone from gaining admittance.

Good job: I thought, allowing myself the beginnings of a smile.

Four insanely fast shots took out four more of the group. I charged two others and cracked their heads together, causing them to drop heavily to the floor.

This left three and the boy.

Two more shots rang out causing a certain amount of non-fatal agony.

One left.

It was the pock-marked thug who we had first encountered in the alley. He was holding the boy close to him and a cruel looking knife was at the youngster's throat. If I had thought that the lad had been scared in the alley, that was nothing compared to what he was radiating now. His heart was galloping faster than a stallion. I couldn't even count the beats as it threatened to burst out of his narrow chest.

"Give us the boy." I spoke as quietly as I could. The situation was still salvageable. "He comes with us. We leave." I gestured to the rest of the group that lay groaning around the room, in pain but otherwise intact. "No one has died."

I held the man's gaze. His eyes were darting around the room: to me, standing with my hands stretched out in a placating manner; to his men lying incapacitated in groups around the floor; to Justice, tall and erect, his pistol stretched out, taking aim.

What did he see?

What did he really see?

Did he see a glimmer of hope? Did he see a way out, a path to a new journey where he could walk away with his life and his dignity?

Did he see monsters drawn up from the lowest pit of Hell, come to mutilate then murder him?

It was as the first drop of blood started to ooze from the youngster's neck that I realised too late there was no hope in this man's eyes at all.

The barrel of Justice's gun flared as I

screamed.

The back of the man's head erupted behind him, spraying blood, bone and grey matter over the wall.

But that did not matter.

Nothing mattered.

Nothing, except the boy.

His life-giving blood oozed out of the savage gash in his neck and soaked into his blue velvet coat — the coat that he had owned for just a few hours. He slumped to the floor, his gizzard gurgling and his skin pale.

I leapt across the space between us and cradled him up into my arms. His heartbeat, formerly so fast, was now ponderous and hesitant. All I could hear, my whole existence, was the faltering footsteps of a drunken man blindly thrashing his way around a darkened room until finally, quickly his tiny form collapsed in a heap: defeated, unconscious.

Dead.

He was gone. This young life, full of wonder and vitality was gone. I was holding an empty shell. The creature inside had slithered away to places unknown.

And there was nothing I could do.

It was all my fault.

Blood streaked down my cheeks as I wept uncontrollably. I buried my face in the boy's hair, desperate to remember the scent of this poor, unfortunate child. I craved oblivion. I cursed the day that Doulos had found me.

Then, through the fog, the haze of unfettered grief, I was aware of a voice.

I looked up at my brother, his face of stone impassive once more and heard him repeat the one word that he had just said: "Leave."

I did not move.

"Go," he said.

I wanted to ask him, "Why?" but I already knew the answer.

I wanted to tell him, "No," but words were precious and never to be wasted. One would never know when one would say one's last.

Carefully, as respectfully as I could, I lay the limp body down on the floor at his father's feet. I walked out of that place, leaving ten wounded men with my grieving brother.

Regent

My cheeks were stained red with sorrow and despair as I sped faster than the human eye could perceive through a town that had assumed the dark mantle of a graveyard for a young innocent. I was aware of inertia spreading the flowing tears across my deathly cold skin. Thin, wet moisture, quite unlike the thick, viscous liquid that had oozed from the boy's throat.

A child who's name I had not even bothered to learn.

My tortured memory saw the scarlet liquid seeping down into the dark blue fabric of his rich velvet jacket — just his for an hour or so. When he had first donned it, his little face had been one of joy. A child with a new toy, something that he would treasure for the rest of his life.

Now it was his shroud — his face pale, lifeless.

My stomach churned and I screeched to a halt, dust rising from the unkempt road upon which I ran. I stumbled to the corner of a deserted building, bent double and vomited onto the packed earth. Coagulating blood pooled around my feet, staining the rich leather of my boots.

Tears joined the mess. I stood, hunched over, crying yet more blood onto the scarlet contents of my now empty stomach.

Blood? In my stomach? How was that even possible? Where did it come from?

There was so much that I still did not understand. So much more to learn.

Like how to create another vampire?

The voice hissed the accusation from the back of my mind.

You could have saved him, like Doulos saved you.

I shook my head and the world blurred. Could I? Could I really have saved him? That wound was so quick, so deep. He was dead in an instant.

But you froze. He called you a princess. You're nothing but a gutter snipe. Trash. Effluent.

"Stop it," I wept. "Please, stop it."

How many more will die because of your mistakes?

"Just stop it." My voice carried more force. I donned an ill-fitting mask of courage as I drew myself up and ignored the continuing roiling of my guts. "I will not listen to you."

But you will, it hissed as it slithered away into the darkest recess of my subconscious. You will.

I stepped back out into the street. It was empty apart from me and my hidden nightmare, the jeering voice from my past, dead life. I needed focus. I craved direction. I closed my eyes, lifted my head and drew in a deep breath.

A familiar scent reached my nostrils.

Doulos, my father. He had been this way.

I ascertained his trail and made haste to follow it.

The scent led me out of town to a cave a reasonable walk past the limits of the tatty urban mass. It was far enough away to be unobserved by human eye, but near enough for our kind to hear anyone approaching.

As my father did when I crested the brow.

He stood out in the open, watching me as I slowed to a walking pace, almost stumbled over my weary feet and staggered into his welcoming arms.

I opened my mouth to speak, to tell him of the awful things that I had witnessed, but no words could adequately describe the scenes that had carved themselves into my memory. The tears tried to flow once more, but I grabbed at them, forced them back inside. I barricaded them within and refused them any grace.

My father, a creature who had seen so much more than I, suffered so much more, just looked down into my distraught visage and nodded.

"The beings we are here to protect," he said, his words doleful, old, tired, "are broken."

"What do you mean?" I managed.

"Think about it. If you knew that you had a protector, someone stronger than you, someone dedicated to you, would you not feel safe? Would you not feel grateful?" He paused as obviously painful memories eased their way from his mind to his mouth. "My mother was not killed by constructs. She was taken, somehow, by a group of humans and burned alive. The very creatures that we were created to protect, tortured and killed their saviour.

"It is their nature. They are creatures of fear, creatures of anger.

"They must never know we exist.

"That is a far too heavy burden."

I stood back from him and studied his face. It

suddenly looked much older than it had earlier in the night. There were lines and creases to his skin that I was sure had not been there just a few hours previous.

Then I noticed the pile of wood. It stood by the entrance to the cave, a mixture of bracken, scrub and dry timbers that had been scavenged from God knew where.

"What is this?" I asked.

Doulos cocked his head and evaded my question. "Your brother approaches," he said. "I would talk to him in private a while. Please, go into that cave and allow me a brief moment to speak to him."

"Father? You didn't answer my question."

"In time, child. In time. You are tired," came the voice that sounded far wearier than my aching body felt. "Go inside and rest."

So I did as I was bid and walked away from my father for the final time.

It was a deep cave and I chose the darkest, most isolated nook that I could find. I wanted to be as far away as possible from the cruel world outside. Settling down onto the uneven floor, I ignored the rough, abrasive stone that dug into my back and I closed my eyes.

I must have drifted off to sleep almost immediately.

I say that because I became aware that I was no longer alone.

There were light footsteps in the dark and my eyes focussed on a figure walking through the gloom. I made to rise but a hand moved in the all-enveloping gloom and gave a calming gesture. "Please, do not get up." The face came into focus and, after a few seconds, recognition dawned.

The neat dark hair; the spectacles. It was the woman from All Saints. The one that the vicar had punished me for talking to.

"Hello Esther," she said.

"Hello, miss." I frowned. "How do you know my name? My mortal name, that is."

A soft smile formed beneath her round spectacles and she hunched down before me. Again, I knew that it must be a dream for it was as if she wasn't really there. Yes, I could see her — her chestnut hair, the dark-rimmed spectacles, the neatly fashioned clothes that she wore — but my other senses balked at what my eyes and ears informed me. There was no scent. My tongue licked my lips and there was no taste of another being's perspiration on the air. My skin felt no movement in the air as she leant forwards towards me in the stillness.

"I know many things," she replied. "Such as the fact that your life is about to be turned upside down once again." Her eyes glanced towards the pinprick of light at the end of the cave before resuming their intimate study of me. "You are so young for what is to befall you. Mind you, I suppose I was not much older, in a certain manner of speaking."

"What are you talking about?" I felt panic start to gnaw at my stomach. Again, I tried to rise, but the stranger lay a hand on my shoulder and eased me back with no effort. Suddenly all panic was gone. Instead, there was warmth, love. In my mind's eye I saw faces. They belonged to my human family: father, mother, brother. They were smiling, pride resonating from them. They saw me and they knew what I was. They approved of what they saw.

"Always be true to what you are and you will

prevail," the woman said. "You have a long journey ahead of you and I am afraid that you will witness terrible things, but you shall also encounter great wonders."

"How can you be so sure?"

"I have already seen them. You will lead your people towards the light of day. Always remember the first things your second father told you."

"Find the Eternals. Protect the Twins. Await the Divergence."

The woman nodded and I was aware of two new sensations. The first was the smell of woodsmoke, drifting in from the entrance to the cave. The second was the noise of tiny wings fluttering around me.

The woman was surrounded by small creatures who were not much bigger than the palm of my hand. Satin wings flitted from their backs, causing them to hover around her shoulders. They were the prettiest little things that I had ever seen. There seemed to be the sound of the tiniest of bells ringing, tintinnabulating as they ducked and dived around my head, looks of curiosity on their faces.

"My companions and I have to go now."

"Must you?" I asked in my dream-like state.

She nodded. "You should go and speak with your brother."

Then she and her little friends were gone and I was alone in the cave.

I blinked, stretched and rubbed my eyes. It had been such a curious dream. It had felt so real, right down to the smell of woodsmoke.

Woodsmoke!

I stood quickly and the smell of burning wood was as real as the kinks in my back. Following it, I ventured to the mouth of the cave just in time to witness the second horror of the night.

My father was stood with my brother in front of a raging bonfire.

He turned.

He leapt.

He burned.

This time there was no holding back the tears. "Why?" I cried.

Justice turned towards me. "He could not carry on."

Staggering forward, I lurched towards my sibling, confusion warping my ability to communicate. Eventually, words formed which I spat out at him: "Why did you not stop him?"

"I could not."

This could not be happening. This was a nightmare. "What are we to do now?" I whispered, wanting nothing more than to be back in the cave, back in my sweet dream.

"You are to carry on."

This pulled me up short. "Me? What about you?" I watched the flames rise higher and higher in the lightening sky. "Surely you are not considering…"

Justice's shoulders rose and fell. "No, nothing like that. I cannot be your king. I am not the right person to rule our kind." He turned and watched the raging flames. "In his cold, dead heart he knew that to be the truth. That is why he created you."

This was not happening.

My family was falling apart.

First the boy, then my father and now my brother.

They were all leaving me. I was an orphan once more — my family dead or deserting me.

This couldn't be happening.

I shook my head, in part to show my disagreement, in part to try and clear the growing fog within. "Me? Really? I think not. I know nothing. You are older. You have seen more. You are the first born."

"I am no ruler," he said. "I can live in the shadows but not with such a burden on my shoulders. I will do my part: furtively, silently. You will hear whispers of my deeds but you will not see me again.

"Not until the time is right.

"Our world is changing at such a rapid pace. People are not ready to know the truth yet of that which goes on right under their noses, but there will come a day when they will be ready — when they will accept that which they thought was fantasy is in fact reality. It shall be a time when I can stand in front of all the peoples of this world and tell them the truth. When that day comes, I shall return. Until then, I shall make sure that justice is served. I shall travel alone and follow my own path.

"Others of our kind will find you. They will see you for what you are: a kind, caring ruler. You shall be their regent whilst their king is in occultation."

You will lead your people towards the light of day. The words wandered through my head. She had known this. She had already seen this. How?

There was so much that I still had to learn.

There was so much that I had to do.

But I wouldn't do it alone. I would search out others of my kind. I would return to England and do what must be done: lead the Children of Cain towards the light of day.

But, right now, the light of day was a dangerous place and, as the sun began its steady rise above the horizon, we retreated into the safe darkness of the cave.

"Justice," I said, "I am afraid."

"As am I," replied my brother. "As am I."

A.S.Chambers

Author's Notes

So, first, an apology. If you've never read any of my books before and have started here, you must be somewhat confused at this moment. All I can say right now is, "Sorry." This one was most definitely a story for my fans and constant readers, those who have been there since day one and have clamoured for more and more details and back story regarding the characters and events in the universe of Sam Spallucci. I hope it encourages you to go away and perhaps start at the beginning with *The Casebook of Sam Spallucci.*

It was while I was writing the fourth Sam Spallucci book, *Dark Justice*, that I realised I wanted to write a back story for Nightingale. This was for a couple of reasons. The first was that, out of all the Children of Cain, she felt the most human, the one that was most easily relatable to. As a result, I enjoyed working with her and my readers were really enjoying her as a character. The second was that her time at All Saints in Wellington was a such a pivotal moment in the universe that I have created. It links in to so many other stories:

Shadows of Lancaster, *Dark Justice*, *Memento* to name but three. The most important link, though, has to be the forthcoming work *Fallen Angel*, the bulk of which will be set in Wellington and centred around the church and, more specifically, the font and what lies beneath.

It was certainly enjoyable to bring in characters from Sam Spallucci's world for their own little cameos. Lucifer is always a joy to work with. (Be prepared to see the installation of the font from his point of view at a later date.) I felt having Marcus as the one who gave Esther her vampire name was a nice touch and set them up as a future partnership. It was wonderful to work with Doulos and Justice one more time. I always find their part of Nightingale's story incredibly emotional for many reasons. I feel that I might not be finished with Doulos yet. He lived a very long time and possibly has a good number of stories to recount of his own.

However, there is one character who I especially loved working with and fleshing out just a tantalisingly bit more: Sophia. I began *Songbird* almost immediately after finishing *Dark Justice*, where I had left Sam on yet another cliffhanger with the primly dressed Sophia revealing that the small fairy-like creatures were in fact angels and that one of them was missing. Whilst writing this novella, I have been starting on the next Sam Spallucci book *Troubled Souls* where she will play a crucial role, so she is currently right at the forefront of my creative mind. Not only this, but she is one of the central figures in the aforementioned *Fallen Angel*. A woman of many secrets, some of which will be revealed in *Troubled Souls*, she was a joy to work with, especially the scene with her and Esther in All Saints.

I had a guide to Victorian England in Pamela

Horn's book from 1975, *The Rise & Fall of The Victorian Servant*. Although young Esther is treated brutally by her employers, the treatment of real life servants was, at times, not too dissimilar. Many employers regarded them as second rate citizens and belongings rather than people in their own rights. On the whole, they worked for a pittance and were nothing more than legalised slaves. There was also the constant fear from the employers, as with the vicar of All Saints, that the young girls that they took into their houses would rob them blind. Indeed many of them did, as Horn recounts. If you can get hold of the book, I highly recommend it as a well-written, engaging and informative read.

A quick word on the church of All Saints. The fictional church is based upon a real one: All Hallows, Wellingborough in Northamptonshire. Wellingborough was a spa town in the 1600s and was visited by Stuart gentry. The church on the marketplace is mediaeval and is laid out exactly as the one in the book: the rood screen, the nave and the font. I spent a number of years there singing in the choir and serving at the altar and it was probably the biggest influence in starting me down my writing path as a teenager. If you are down that way at some point, I highly recommend that you visit it.

My last word is on the Bare Lane Butcher, as mentioned twice by Esther's employers. Let's just say, you'll need to read the forthcoming *Sam Spallucci: Troubled Souls* for more enlightenment on that topic...

A.S.Chambers.
May 2019.

ABOUT THE AUTHOR

A.S.Chambers resides in Lancaster, England. He lives a fairly simple life measuring the growing rates of radishes and occasionally puts pen to paper to stop the voices in his head from constantly berating him.

He is quite happy for, and in fact would encourage, you to follow him on Facebook, Instagram and Twitter.

There is also a nice, shiny website:
www.aschambers.co.uk

Printed in Poland
by Amazon Fulfillment
Poland Sp. z o.o., Wrocław